PUFFIN BOOKS

THE MAN FROM THE EGG

Sudha Murty was born in 1950 in Shiggaon, north Karnataka. She did her MTech in computer science, and is now the chairperson of the Infosys Foundation. A prolific writer in English and Kannada, she has written novels, technical books, travelogues, collections of short stories and non-fictional pieces, and six bestselling books for children: Her books have been translated into all the major Indian languages. Sudha Murty is the recipient of the R.K. Narayan Award for Literature (2006), the Padma Shri (2006) and the Attimabbe Award from the Government of Karnataka for excellence in Kannada literature (2011).

Also in Puffin by Sudha Murty

*How I Taught My Grandmother to Read and
Other Stories*
The Magic Drum and Other Favourite Stories
The Bird with Golden Wings
Grandma's Bag of Stories
The Magic of the Lost Temple
*The Serpent's Revenge: Unusual Tales from
the Mahabharata*

SUDHA MURTY

THE MAN FROM THE EGG

Unusual Tales about the TRINITY

Illustrations by Priyankar Gupta

PUFFIN BOOKS

An imprint of Penguin Random House

PUFFIN BOOKS

USA | Canada | UK | Ireland | Australia
New Zealand | India | South Africa | China

Puffin Books is part of the Penguin Random House group of companies
whose addresses can be found at global.penguinrandomhouse.com

Published by Penguin Random House India Pvt. Ltd
7th Floor, Infinity Tower C, DLF Cyber City,
Gurgaon 122 002, Haryana, India

Penguin
Random House
India

First published in Puffin Books by Penguin Random House India 2017

Text copyright © Sudha Murty 2017
Illustrations copyright © Priyankar Gupta 2017

All rights reserved

10 9 8 7 6 5 4 3 2 1

ISBN 9780143427865

Typeset in Dante MT Std by Manipal Digital Systems, Manipal
Printed at Replika Press Pvt. Ltd, India

www.penguin.co.in

To Kris Gopalakrishnan and Sudha,
for the precious memories made during the making of Infosys

Contents

Introduction   ix

OMKARA SWARUPA

1. Brahma's Folly   3
2. A Celestial Solution   7

SATYAM SHIVAM SUNDARAM

3. The Story of Sati   15
4. The Birth of Parvati   19
5. The Indian Cupid   24
6. A Match Made in Heaven   30
7. The Moon and the Leaf   34
8. The Legends of the Elephant God   39
9. The Slaying of the Asuras   47
10. The Half-Man, Half-Woman   55
11. Folk Tales   58

SAMBHAVAMI YUGE YUGE

12. The Bones of Dadhichi   77
13. The Churning of the Ocean   80

14. The Ten Avatars   87
15. Three Mortal Lifetimes   101
16. A Friend in Need   115
17. The Man from the Egg   123
18. The Forked Tongues   129
19. The Honest Cheater   134
20. The Choice of Death   139
21. To Marry a Monkey or a Bear   143
22. The Web of Illusion   149
23. The Debt for a Wedding   154
24. The Asura and the Super-God   164

Notes   167

Introduction

87
101
115
123
129
134
120

In India, the term Trimurti is used in reference to the three faces of god. They are Brahma, Vishnu and Shiva, and collectively called the Trinity.

Together, they represent the oneness of the universe while retaining their distinctive nature and are known for their ability to grant people boons. Hymns are chanted every day all over India, in temples and homes, and countless stories abound in their praise.

And yet many questions remain.

Several temples are dedicated to Shiva, as well as Vishnu and his various avatars. But there are hardly any that are dedicated to Brahma, an equally important part of the Trinity. Why?

How do the demons or asuras attempt to cheat the Trinity in their endless quest for immortality? How do their efforts fail?

Saraswati, Lakshmi and Parvati are the respective consorts of Brahma, Vishnu and Shiva. But it is Parvati who displays many avatars and is popular as Shakti, the divine female power, and Durga, the warrior goddess. How did Parvati, a beautiful and gentle being, come to be known as a feared warrior?

This is the second volume of my series on Indian mythology, written for my dear readers and for future generations.

As always, I would like to thank my wonderful editor Shrutkeerti Khurana and Anju Kulkarni for their roles in bringing out this book. I am also grateful to Sohini Mitra and Hemali Sodhi from Penguin for their support and belief in me.

Omkara Swarupa

Brahma's Folly

Lord Brahma is the creator of the universe and everything both living and non-living. He is said to have risen from a lotus that emerged from Vishnu's belly button. Just as an artisan moulds statues, Brahma is the eternal sculptor responsible for the intricacies of all life forms. We are all his children.

Ages ago, the god of love, Manmatha (better known today as Kamadeva), and his wife, Rati, prayed fervently to Brahma for a boon. They wanted a special bow and arrow. So they fasted and meditated for days and days, and finally Brahma appeared.

Manmatha said, 'Dear lord, give me a bow and arrow that will make anyone I shoot it with fall instantly in love with the nearest person.'

Brahma considered the request. 'This boon is perfect!' he thought. 'It will encourage more humans to fall in love and over time, the number of children on this planet will increase and the human race will flourish. But I don't think strong-willed people or those who follow a spiritual path will fall prey to Manmatha's arrow. However, that shouldn't stop me from granting the boon.'

Brahma raised his right hand. 'So be it.'

A bow of sugar cane and an arrow of flowers appeared in front of the delighted Manmatha. He took possession of it and thanked the god with all his heart before going on his way.

Soon, Manmatha wanted to test the bow and arrow. Without thinking too much, he shot the first arrow at Brahma himself!

At that time, Brahma was in the process of creating a beautiful maiden. She was named Shatarupa, a woman with a hundred beautiful forms. Her beauty was nothing like the world had ever seen.

As soon as Brahma finished breathing life into her, the magic of Manmatha's arrow started to take effect.

The lord began gazing at Shatarupa so intensely that it scared her. She hadn't expected her creator to behave in such a manner. So she stepped away from him, turning to his right. Brahma couldn't look away—his eyes followed her. To his surprise, a second head sprang up on his right. Alarmed, Shatarupa ran the other way, to his left, but a third head appeared in that direction as well. Finally, Shatarupa was right behind Brahma, and lo and behold, another head was formed. Now Brahma had four heads facing all four directions—east, west, north and south. This way he was able to see Shatarupa no matter where she went.

The maiden now had no choice but to turn upward. Unfortunately for her, that didn't stop Brahma. Another head facing the sky sprang up on his first head. And thus Brahma's gaze stayed on Shatarupa.

Shiva, who had been watching the entire incident, was furious. 'It is time for me to step in and help the poor girl,' he

thought. 'Brahma is Shatarupa's creator—it is not right for him to fall in love with her like this.'

Shiva cut off Lord Brahma's sky-facing head in one swoop with his *trishul* and cast a curse on him. 'Henceforth, you will eternally be a four-headed god, and furthermore, you will be worshipped in just one place.'

Only after he had removed Brahma's fifth head did Shiva realize that Brahma hadn't been completely responsible for his behaviour. It was Manmatha's arrow of love that had started it all.

So, to soften the curse, Shiva declared, 'Brahma, even though you may not be worshipped the way Vishnu and I are, you will always be revered as a part of the divine Trinity.'

There was no denying that Shiva had sinned by punishing Brahma. As a consequence, he became a wandering ascetic and made his way to Brahma Kapala (better known today as Badrinath in Uttarakhand). Shiva carried Brahma's severed head in his hands and used it as a begging bowl, but strangely the skull would never fill up. No matter how much food went into it, the bowl remained empty. It was only when Shiva made his way to Varanasi and received alms from Annapoorna, the goddess of nourishment and an avatar of Parvati, that the begging bowl finally began to fill up. It is believed that Brahma's fifth head has remained with Shiva ever since.

The place where this incident is said to have taken place is in Pushkar, Rajasthan.

A Celestial Solution

The asura brothers Sunda and Upasunda were inseparable. They shared everything equally—food, clothes, even their kingdom.

In the hope of gaining immortality, they performed severe penance to please Brahma. After a long time, the god finally appeared.

'We are overjoyed to be in your presence, my lord!' they said, bowing to Brahma.

'Your penance is commendable, my dear devotees.' Brahma smiled. 'I will grant you a boon. Tell me, what do you wish for?'

Sunda and Upasunda had been waiting for this moment. 'We want to be immortal,' they chorused.

'I'm afraid that is impossible. Any living being that is born must die. I am only the creator, and have no power to stop death. Ask me for something else instead.'

After careful thought, Sunda and Upasunda said, 'Then give us such a boon that will allow us to die only by each other's hand and no other.'

Now, Brahma was famous for granting boons to his asura devotees. More often than not, there were strange conditions

associated with these boons. The truth was that Brahma
made sure to weave loopholes into his boons, knowing
that every mortal must die. This time was no different. He
nodded and said, 'May you be invincible from this day on.
You can only be killed by each other.'

Sunda and Upasunda were ecstatic. They knew that they
would never fight each other.

Together, the brothers conquered many lands and
became immensely powerful. Their invincibility made them
arrogant, and they soon started to abuse their subjects. Friends
and enemies alike feared them because they were known to
seize kingdoms on a whim. After decades of suffering their
torture, the whole world wanted to see the brothers dead but
the bond between them remained as strong as ever. They
didn't seem to have a single difference of opinion!

Finally, the people appealed to Brahma. 'Please rid the
world of these monsters. We have no one else to turn to,'
they pleaded.

'All powerful asuras inevitably turn towards the
destruction of mankind,' thought Brahma as he listened to
the people's relentless cries for help. 'As I'm the one who
bestowed the boon of invincibility upon them and caused
this misery, it is my responsibility to find a solution.'

After much thinking, Brahma hit upon an ingenious
plan. He created a beautiful and irresistible enchantress and
named her Tilottama.

Tilottama, by Brahma's design, ran into Sunda and
Upasunda during one of their strolls. The brothers were
immediately captivated by her magical beauty. She nodded
at them as she walked past.

Sunda stared at Tilottama in wonder and said to his brother, 'I want to marry her.'

Upasunda did not reply. He was thinking the same thing!

Sunda noticed his brother gazing at his future wife and realized what was going on in his mind. 'This exquisite woman is going to be Upasunda's sister-in-law!' he thought. 'How dare he stare at her in this manner?' He barked at his brother, 'Come to your senses. She is going to be my wife. You must treat her like a sister.'

'But I was the one who saw her first! She must marry *me*,' replied Upasunda.

'How can you say that, brother?'

'Listen to me. The moment our eyes met, I knew we were meant for each other.'

Sunda did not agree. 'I am the older sibling. I am to marry her and my decision is final.'

'Just because you are older doesn't mean you can force your choices on me. My opinion matters too.'

This rankled Sunda. Gradually the argument between the brothers escalated. Neither of the asuras was ready to relinquish Tilottama. After much debate, they decided to approach the maiden herself to ask her whom *she* liked best, agreeing to respect her choice no matter what.

When the asuras explained the conundrum to Tilottama, she pretended to be upset. 'I curse my beauty!' she exclaimed. 'It has caused a rift between the two of you. It is better that I leave your kingdom.'

'No, Tilottama, please don't leave,' they pleaded. 'Be honest with us. Whom would you like to be wedded to?'

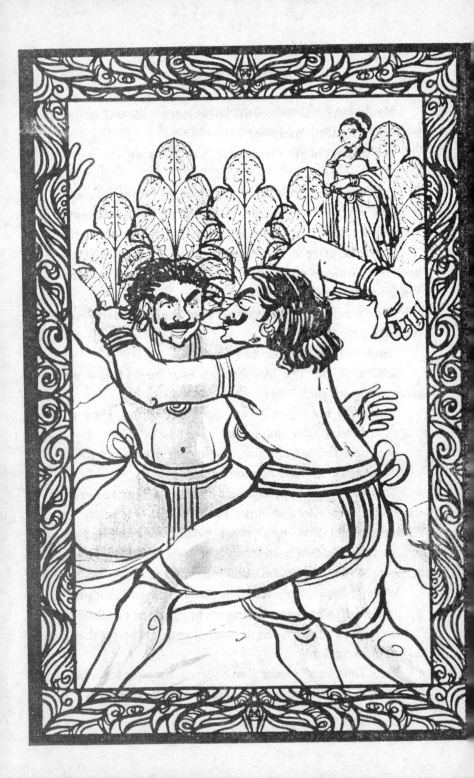

'My dream is to marry the greatest warrior on earth,' she said coyly. 'So I will wed whoever is stronger, but I will leave that to you both to decide.'

Sunda and Upasunda forgot everything except their love for Tilottama. They decided to have a wrestling match. The news spread like wildfire. Many people, animals, birds and even devas swarmed to the scene.

The match was fierce and intense as the brothers were equal in strength. Sunda and Upasunda were aware of each other's weaknesses and fought viciously like two enraged elephants as the world watched with bated breath. In the end, neither of them survived.

Everyone rejoiced and Brahma smiled. What could never have been put an end to by might was easily undone by beauty.

Satyam Shivam Sundaram

The Story of Sati

King Daksha was one of the sons of Lord Brahma. Daksha had many daughters. Twenty-seven of them were married to the handsome moon god, Chandra, and among his remaining daughters, Dakshayani was married to Shiva.

Daksha was not at all happy with Dakshayani's choice. Shiva spent most of his time either on Mount Kailash in the freezing Himalayas or in cremation grounds. To make matters worse, he looked positively dreadful with his long, dark, matted locks and that snake wrapped around his neck like a garland. Daksha felt that his beautiful daughter deserved a better husband. But Dakshayani (who was also known as Rudrani) was very happy with her husband and enjoyed her time with him no matter where they were.

One day, Daksha decided to perform a grand yagna. He invited all his daughters and his sons-in-law, as well as many other relatives and friends to participate in the event.

On the day of the yagna, as soon as Daksha entered the place, everyone stood up to welcome him. All except Brahma and Shiva.

Daksha was livid. God or not, Shiva was his son-in-law. And by not standing up at his arrival, Shiva had insulted Daksha—at least that's how the king perceived it.

A few months later, Daksha held another grand yagna. But this time, he didn't invite Dakshayani and Shiva. When Dakshayani heard that all her sisters were visiting her father's house, she said to Shiva, 'I want to go to my father's house for the yagna. Will you come with me?'

Shiva smiled and replied, 'You shouldn't go without an invitation, even if it is your father's home.'

'A daughter doesn't need an invitation to visit her parents,' she retorted.

'All right, but be warned that your father may use strong words against me. I know how loyal and kind you are, and I'm afraid that it may be hard for you to listen to him. I hope you will be careful. I won't accompany you, dear wife, but my blessings are with you.'

Dakshayani quickly collected a few gifts and left for Daksha's house with Nandi, Shiva's gentle white bull and his primary vehicle.

When Daksha saw his daughter, he said, 'I don't remember having sent you an invitation. Is your ill-mannered husband also going to turn up later?'

Dakshayani didn't say anything, barely restraining her anger.

The yagna began, but Daksha wasn't done ridiculing Shiva. 'Go back, dear daughter, to your husband, whom you love more than your father. I remember his insult very well, and both of you are no longer welcome here.'

He continued in this vein until Dakshayani couldn't take it any longer. Humiliated beyond words, she closed her eyes

Sudha Murty

and prayed to her husband, 'My lord, I have made a mistake by coming here and not heeding your warning. You were right. And I cannot live with the scars of the words my father has inflicted on me.' She then jumped into the sacred fire of the yagna, thus performing the act of sati.

A disturbed silence fell over the room. All the guests were shocked at what had just happened.

When Shiva learnt of his wife's fate, he cried out in such anger that the entire world shook. In his rage, he created a fearsome avatar, Virabhadra, and provided him with a forceful army. He then ordered Virabhadra to stop Daksha's ritual and destroy anyone who stood in his way.

His grief and fury not quelled yet, Shiva began his divine dance of destruction, Tandav Nritya. The earth quaked in the wake of his wrathful steps and people started panicking, convinced that the world was about to end. But Shiva didn't stop or falter.

Meanwhile, Virabhadra and his army destroyed the yagna. He cut off Daksha's head and vanquished the other sages and gods who came forward to help the king. As the destruction continued, they called upon Brahma for help, who entreated Shiva to pardon Daksha and restore normalcy to the world.

Finally Shiva calmed down, his compassion awakened. He brought Daksha back to life, replacing his head with that of a goat's so the proud king would never forget his folly. Daksha immediately fell at Shiva's feet, vowing to spend the rest of his life as his devotee.

Once order was restored in the world, Shiva withdrew into himself and entered a state of deep meditation. And Dakshayani came to be known as Sati from then on.

The Birth of Parvati

Taraka was a powerful and ambitious asura, and a devotee of Lord Brahma. One day he began a severe penance for Brahma, living on a mountain for a long period of time. Pleased with Taraka's devotion, the creator appeared before him.

'O my lord!' Taraka cried. 'My life's purpose has been fulfilled now that I have felt your presence.'

Brahma smiled. 'Tell me what your heart desires.'

'I want to live forever,' replied Taraka.

'My dearest devotee, you know that such a boon is not possible. Why don't you ask me for something else?'

Taraka thought for some time. 'I don't want to die at the hands of just any man or god. If I must perish, I would rather it happened at the hands of the son of Shiva,' he said, knowing full well that Shiva, grief-stricken by the loss of Dakshayani, was far from even the thought of marrying again. So the boon would actually make Taraka invincible and keep him safe from Yama, the god of death.

Brahma understood Taraka's intention. Nevertheless, he said, 'So may it be.'

His penance now complete, Taraka descended from the mountain and returned to his abode. Over time, he created a powerful army headed by ten cruel generals. And then he went on a rampage, conquering kingdoms, abusing living beings on earth as well as the gods above. He terrorized them all so much that everyone began praying to Lord Vishnu.

Vishnu heard their pleas. 'Shiva and Parvati's son will be the cause of Taraka's doom,' he declared.

Himavat or Parvatraj, the king of the Himalayas, had a wife named Menaka. The queen really wanted a daughter who would grow up to become Shiva's consort. When Menaka heard about Dakshayani, she instinctively knew that Shiva's wife would be reborn as her daughter. She thus decided to go into deep meditation, convinced that destiny would soon take its course.

Menaka gave birth to a beautiful baby girl, whom she named Uma. As Uma was the daughter of Parvatraj, she was also known as Parvati, or Himani (from her father's other name, Himavat), or Girija (meaning the daughter of the king of mountains), or Shailaja (meaning the daughter of the mountains).[1]

Parvati was a charming child and unusually devoted to Shiva right from her birth. Even as an adult, she was always

---

[1] In olden times, daughters usually got their names from their fathers' names or the kingdoms they belonged to. For instance, in the Ramayana, King Janaka's daughter, Sita, was popularly known as Janaki. Her other names include Vaidehi (derived from Videha, her father's kingdom) and Maithili (from Mithila, the capital of Videha). Similarly, in the Mahabharata, King Drupada's daughter was called Draupadi or Panchali, as Drupada ruled over the kingdom of Panchala.

found either praying to Shiva or just talking about him. News of her beauty and intelligence spread far and wide. Though suitors came in hordes with the hope of winning her heart, Parvati could only think of Shiva and refused to entertain the idea of marrying anyone else.

The devas were watching all this with great interest. They eagerly awaited the arrival of Parvati and Shiva's son—the harbinger of Taraka's death.

Shiva, on the other hand, deep in meditation atop the cold Mount Kailash, remained unaware of what was going on. Much to the concern of her parents, a determined Parvati made the arduous journey to Kailash and began serving Shiva. She took care of his surroundings, brought him fruits and made garlands for him every day. She wanted to be there the moment he opened his eyes so they could marry as soon as possible.

The gods sighed with relief and hoped that Shiva would soon awaken from his penance.

Days, months and years passed but Shiva showed no signs of emerging from his meditation. If he did not open his eyes, he would never see Parvati, which meant that he wouldn't marry her or have a son. And if the current state of affairs continued, Taraka's cruel reign would be the end of everybody.

Frustrated, the gods decided to take matters into their own hands. All the realms were in grave danger. They had to intervene and force Shiva to awaken, but who would take the risk? No one dared offer to be the one to disturb Shiva's penance and become the target of his infamous temper. Everyone knew that when he was extremely angry, his

third eye would open and immediately spew a great fire that destroyed everything in its path.

And yet the task needed to be done.

The gods decided to approach the diplomatic Lord Vishnu and beseech him to find a way to guarantee Shiva and Parvati's marriage.

'All right, let's see how things turn out,' Vishnu said with a mysterious smile.

The Indian Cupid

The god and goddess of eternal love, Manmatha and Rati, were a lovely couple. Their affection for each other blossomed visibly during the spring season, and their companions included flowers, buds, cuckoos, parrots, honeybees and lush green trees.

One day, Manmatha's father,[2] Vishnu, summoned him to his abode and said, 'I have a difficult task for you. You are the only god with the ability to wake Shiva from his stupor. Once you do that, he will open his eyes and see the beautiful Parvati. As you are the god of love, you must use the power of your gentle arrows to make him fall in love with her.'

An alarmed Manmatha replied, 'Dear Father, you are asking me to play with fire. Shiva is no ordinary god! He is the lord of destruction! His temper is fearsome . . . and you know what will happen if he opens his fiery third eye. Didn't you see his Tandav Nritya after Dakshayani jumped into fire? Even *you* couldn't pacify him. And Lord Brahma just about managed to calm him down before he destroyed the whole

---

[2] In some versions, Brahma is considered to be Manmatha's father.

world. So how do you think *I* can withstand his wrath? I fear this will be the end of me. Please let me go.'

Vishnu then said sternly, 'Manmatha, there's no denying that Shiva can be ferocious, but don't forget that he is also exceptionally kind. He forgave his father-in-law and brought him back to life. He is the only god who grants boons to his devotees irrespective of the cost to himself—that's how much his followers mean to him. Even if something unfortunate were to happen, trust me, he'll be the first to save you. This is no ordinary task—the fate of the world rests on it.'

But Manmatha and Rati were still hesitant.

'It is your duty!' insisted Vishnu. 'Taraka has become such a huge menace that nobody wants to challenge him. The world is suffering, Manmatha, and if you don't make Shiva fall in love with Parvati, he will neither marry her nor produce the son fated to bring about Taraka's death. The asura will continue to torment every living being, and you will be the only one responsible for it!'

Manmatha understood that he had no choice in the matter.

He reluctantly made his way to Mount Kailash with Rati. There they saw Parvati gazing lovingly at Shiva, who was deep in meditation, unaware of her presence.

Manmatha got to work. He called upon all of his companions for help, which included his vehicle (a parrot), a swarm of humming honeybees and Vasantha, the god of spring. Within minutes, the cold and harsh Mount Kailash was transformed into a magical land in springtime. The ice melted and streams of cool blue water began to flow melodically. The frost-covered leaves changed to a brilliant reddish green that shone in the light of the sun as the birds started chirping and singing. The air was filled with a heady fragrance as buds bloomed into brightly coloured flowers. The whole scene was perfect for some romance.

But nothing happened. Shiva remained oblivious to his surroundings.

Rati and Manmatha didn't give up that easily. Being accomplished dancers, they put up an enthralling performance in front of the motionless Shiva.

He still didn't stir.

Parvati, on the other hand, was enchanted by the beauty of the setting. She prayed fervently to Shiva to open his eyes.

Days went by with no luck.

Manmatha became increasingly restless. None of his schemes were working. As a last resort, he picked up his bow of sugar cane and five flowered arrows. Each arrow was tipped with a different kind of flower—white lotus, blue lotus, jasmine, mango blossom and a flower from the ashoka tree. These arrows were so potent that the slightest contact with any of them was enough for most to immediately fall madly in love with the nearest person.

Manmatha shot Shiva with all five arrows at once, which gently touched the god and fell to the ground. Shiva's eyes fluttered open. He stared ahead without blinking, his eyes burning with incandescent rage. 'Who dares disturb my penance?' he thought.

And then he saw Manmatha, who smiled at him in the hope of a friendly response. As Shiva was silent, Manmatha

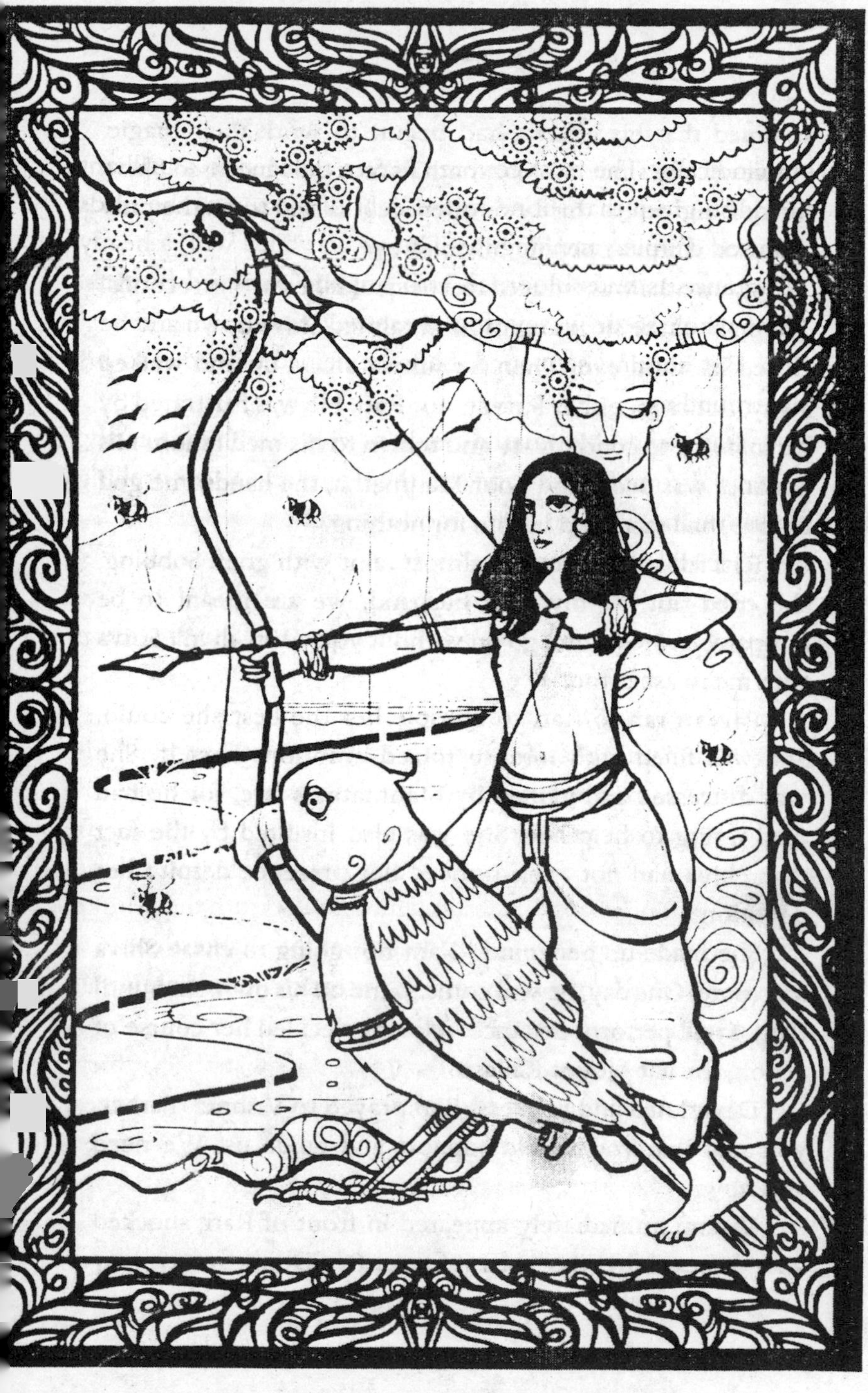

assumed that his arrows had begun to work their magic. However, the smile on Manmatha's face only incensed Shiva further, and so his third eye opened. It is said to be the only instance of Shiva opening his third eye.

Manmatha was reduced to a heap of ashes within seconds. The sight of the steaming mound calmed Shiva down and he closed his third eye. Then he simply stood up and walked away, noticing neither Parvati nor Rati. He was frustrated by his inability to concentrate and return to his meditation. His penance was over. And poor Manmatha, the handsome god of love, had sacrificed his life for nothing.

Rati fell to the ground, almost faint with grief. Sobbing, she cried out, 'O my dear husband, we are meant to be inseparable. How can I go on without you? Why didn't Shiva turn me to ashes too?'

Parvati ran to Rati to console her the best she could. She was filled with intense mixed emotions herself. She was distressed and pained by Manmatha's fate, for he had died trying to help her! She was also insulted by the fact that Shiva had not even noticed her presence despite her devotion!

She made up her mind. 'I am not going to chase Shiva any more. One day, he will come to me on his own. And until then, I will perform penance.' Having decided her course of action, she left Mount Kailash.

Devastated and helpless, Rati prayed to Vishnu, 'Father, you said that you would support and guide us. We need you now.'

Vishnu immediately appeared in front of Rati, shocked and dejected by the turn of events. 'Don't worry, my daughter,' he said. 'I will revive Manmatha, though he will no longer possess the human form. He will arise in the thoughts of people, and you will remain inseparable. Whoever thinks about love will inevitably invoke you and Manmatha. He will henceforth be known as Manoj, "the one who emerges from the mind", or Ananga, "the one without a body". The whole world will remember both your sacrifices.'

This incident, the burning of Manmatha, is associated with Holi,[3] which is usually followed by a light drizzle the next day. The rain is believed to be made up of the tears that Rati shed on the loss of her husband.

---

[3] The celebration of Holi is also attributed to the mythological tale of Prahlada, a *daitya* king.

A Match Made in Heaven

A determined Parvati began her penance, abstaining from food and only focusing on her chanting, which earned her the name Aparna, or 'the girl who refuses to eat even a leaf'. With each passing day, her *tapasya* became more and more severe, until the entire world was aware of her meditation. Years passed, and Parvati grew powerful with the strength she obtained from her intense penance.

In the meantime, Shiva came to learn about everything that had transpired—her devotion to him and his failure to notice her. He realized that she wasn't a mere mortal, and decided to test her faith.

Shiva approached Parvati disguised as a sanyasi begging for food. Though she was deep in meditation, she sensed the sanyasi's presence and opened her eyes. A wave of peace and calm swept over Shiva.

Parvati stared at him without realizing who he was, and then offered him all she had. While receiving the alms, the ascetic asked, 'Why are you performing this penance?'

'It is for Shiva. I wish to marry him,' she said simply.

'But he is not worthy of you, my lady,' said the ascetic. 'Shiva's dwelling is atop the cold and bleak Mount Kailash, and sometimes he's even found in cremation grounds. You are exquisite and refined while his appearance is ghoulish. He smears ash on his body and uses skulls for garlands. You are delicate while he is slovenly. You are sweet-tempered while Shiva is known for his wrath. He is no match for you. You should marry someone kind, handsome and gentle, who can treat you the way you deserve to be treated. Take my sincere advice and end your penance. Go back to the life that you were meant to live.'

Parvati was furious at the sanyasi's words. 'You came to me for food and I have given you all that I can. It is time for you to be on your way. I know Shiva's soul. He does not care for fine clothes and ornaments. Why, he doesn't even care for grand rituals performed in his name! A devotee can offer him a leaf from a bael tree and some water, and he would be satisfied. He is the kindest of all the gods, and he always stands by the promises he makes to his followers, regardless of who they are. I am sorry, but I do not need your guidance in this matter.'

The ascetic, however, paid no heed to her words. He continued, 'But, my lady, what about the way he reduced poor Manmatha to a heap of ashes . . . surely you can't approve of that—'

'I cannot listen to you any more! And if you won't leave, I will,' Parvati retorted.

Just as she turned to go, there was a flash of white light and Shiva appeared in his true form.

'My dear Parvati,' he said. 'Please forgive me for my harsh words. It is my loss that I was unaware of your presence earlier. But I can see you clearly now. You are Dakshayani, my beloved consort, and we belong together. We always have. Will you marry me and agree to be my companion for eternity?'

Parvati smiled and nodded in assent.

The whole world rejoiced when they heard the news, and the wedding, which was known as Girija Kalyana, was celebrated with much pomp and show.

In time, a child was born to the couple, whom they named Karthikeya. He was also called Shanmukha because he had six faces, which meant that he could see problems approaching from anywhere.

Karthikeya knew the purpose of his birth. While he was still a child, he fought the mighty Taraka with the support of the gods and eventually slew him using his most deadly weapon—Shakti. He also killed Taraka's two brothers: Simhamukhan, who later became Parvati's mount, and Suradpadman, who was reborn as the peacock that became Karthikeya's vehicle.

News of his valour spread far and wide, and the gods eventually appointed him as commander of the heavenly army.

Thus, Karthikeya's birth ended Taraka's cruel reign and saved the world.

The Moon and the Leaf

The Origin of the Crescent Moon

According to legend, the moon god, Chandra, was born three times, which is why he also came to be known as Trijanmi. The first time, he was created by Brahma, and the second time, he emerged from the eyes of Sage Atri. Chandra's radiance became so powerful and intolerable that he was immersed in an ocean of milk to ensure the world's survival. During another event, which involved the churning of the ocean by the asuras and the devas, Chandra was reborn and released, along with Goddess Lakshmi. Thus, Chandra came to be known as Lakshmi's brother.

Among his twenty-seven wives, Daksha's daughters, Chandra was especially fond of his fourth wife, Rohini, and spent most of his time with her. The other wives resented his indifference to them and complained about it to their father. Daksha immediately cursed Chandra. 'May your powers decline with the passing of each day,' he said, losing his temper as usual.

34

Now the daughters regretted telling Daksha what they had. Their intention was not to punish Chandra—all they wanted was his attention. What if their husband simply disappeared one day along with his powers?

Chandra begged Daksha to take the curse back. But once a curse is uttered, no one can revoke it. 'I am sorry, son,' Daksha said. 'There is nothing that I can do now. Perhaps if you pray to Shiva, he may help you.'

Holding on to this slim ray of hope, Chandra went to the famed holy ground Prabhas Patan, established a linga and prayed earnestly to Shiva. Pleased with Chandra's devotion, Shiva appeared and said, 'Chandra, I empathize with your plight and, though I cannot reverse Daksha's curse, I can soften it to some extent. From this day onward, you will increase in brightness for fifteen days in Shukla Paksha[4] and then wane for fifteen days in Krishna Paksha.[5] You will fill the world with your radiance on full moon days and disappear on new moon days.'

Chandra was disappointed at the thought of waxing and waning. His crescent shape would just be a constant reminder of the curse and his reduced strength! Shiva consoled him by saying, 'My dear child, the crescent indicates that you will still retain some of your powers. I will wear your crescent in my hair to show my devotees that they are dear to me even in their lowest moments. That way you will be my constant companion.'

---

[4] The fortnight between a new moon day and a full moon day is called Shukla Paksha.
[5] The fortnight between a full moon day and a new moon day is called Krishna Paksha.

Thus Shiva came to be known as Chandrasekhar, or 'the one with Chandra mounted on his head'.

The moon came to be known as Soma and one day of the week—Somavar or Monday—was dedicated to him. The linga that Chandra worshipped became famous as the pilgrimage site of Somnath in Gujarat. Generous donations were made to this site, which was later plundered seventeen times. This linga is considered to be the first *jyotirlinga*[6] in our country.

These twenty-seven wives of Chandra are the constellations surrounding the moon's orbit, and are frequently referred to as nakshatras or stars. The names of these nakshatras—for example, Kritika, Rohini and Ashwini—are still an important part of the Hindu calendar.

The Origin of Bilva

Mandara the mountain was a great devotee of Parvati because of her kindness and the fact that she was the daughter of the king of mountains. Parvati lived with her husband, Shiva, on Mount Kailash but Mandara longed for her presence on his mountain.

One day, Shiva and Parvati danced for many hours on end. Finally tired, Parvati stopped to rest, wiping the sweat

---

[6] The jyotirlinga is an iconic representation of Shiva. It is said to have emitted light.

off her forehead with her hand. The droplets fell on Mandara and a sapling sprang up there, growing taller and stronger until it became a beautiful tree within a few months. Nobody had ever seen this tree before. Each of its twigs sprouted three leaves and it also bore fruit.

Mandara took some twigs to Parvati. When he met her, he asked, 'This tree was born of your sweat. What must I do with it?'

Parvati looked at the twigs and the leaves thoughtfully. 'What a wonderful tree!' she exclaimed. 'The three leaves indicate the three eyes of Lord Shiva and the three stages of all existence—birth, the journey of life and death. They also represent the three realms—heaven, earth and the world below. So three is an auspicious number.'

She beamed at Mandara and continued, 'Your faith and devotion pleases me. This tree will be called the Bilva tree and the leaves, Bilva *patra*. Everyone must pray to Shiva with these leaves. And since we are inseparable, worshipping Shiva in this manner also means worshipping me. You will always have the Bilva tree on your mountain.'

Mandara couldn't contain his happiness and prostrated himself before the beautiful goddess. His prayers had been answered.

This is why Bilva leaves are used as an offering to Shiva even today.

The Legends of the Elephant God

The God of Knowledge

One day, Parvati happened to observe all the followers around Shiva from their abode on Mount Kailash. She remarked, 'These people are all your devotees, my lord. They listen only to you and not to me.'

'That can't be true, Parvati,' replied Shiva.

Parvati did not say anything further, but she was convinced that she was right.

A few days later, she called for Shiva's white bull and said to him, 'Nandi, I am going to take a bath. Please guard the door and make sure no one comes in till I am done.'

When Shiva came home, he saw Nandi standing guard outside. 'Where is Parvati?' he asked.

'She is taking a bath.'

Shiva nodded and tried to step inside but Nandi stopped him, saying, 'My lord, the goddess has ordered me not to allow anyone in until she is ready.'

'That may be so, Nandi, but this is my house and I am your lord and her husband. I can go in and out as I please.'

Convinced, Nandi moved aside and allowed Shiva to enter.

When Parvati saw Shiva, she realized that Nandi was more loyal to his master than to her. She was overwhelmed by sadness, for she wanted somebody who'd be as faithful to her and follow her instructions without question.

The next time Parvati wanted to bathe, instead of relying on someone else to guard her door, she decided to create a new person altogether. She sculpted the statue of a young boy with some mud and breathed life into him. She named him Ganesha.

As soon as Ganesha came to life, he bowed and said, 'Mother, I am here to do your bidding. Tell me, how may I help you today?'

Parvati said gently, 'My child, I am going to take a bath. Please don't allow anyone inside the house until I am done.'

Some time passed and Shiva came home. He was surprised to see the little boy standing guard outside his house.

'Little one, who are you? Where are your parents and why are you standing here?' asked Shiva.

The boy replied boldly, 'My name is Ganesha and I am Parvati's son.'

Shiva did not believe him. 'Move aside and let me enter,' he said.

'No, I cannot do that. I must follow my mother's orders. Please wait out here with me until she is done.'

'Little boy, don't you know who I am? I am Shiva and this is *my* home. You cannot stop me from entering my own home.'

But Ganesha refused to be intimidated. He repeated, 'I am sorry, but I can't allow you inside until my mother says it is all right to do so.'

Ganesha's response irritated Shiva. He tried to reason with him again and again, but the boy would not budge.

Finally, Shiva lost his temper and cut off Ganesha's head with a single swish of his trishul. The sheer force of the blow sent the boy's head flying out of the Himalayas.

Hearing the commotion, Parvati rushed outside, but it was too late. Her child's headless body lay on the white icy ground before her. Parvati cried out in despair and anger, 'This is my son . . . . my beloved child! Who has dared to do this to him?'

By now Shiva had realized his folly. Feeling extremely remorseful for what he had done, he tried to console Parvati, saying, 'I have made a huge mistake. I did not know that you had created him—I thought he was lying about being your son. Please forgive me—I will do everything I can to revive him.'

Though her face remained streaked with tears, Parvati looked at Ganesha's body and nodded silently.

Shiva then instructed Nandi to go north and find the boy's head.

Nandi looked for the head everywhere, but in vain. He returned to Shiva and said, 'My lord, the head is nowhere to be found. What should I do?'

'Try again, Nandi,' insisted Shiva. 'Or . . . if you find anyone sleeping with his head towards the north, please remove their head and bring it to me.'

Nandi rushed out to follow his master's orders. He finally saw an elephant sleeping with its head towards the north. Without a moment's hesitation, Nandi cut it off and brought it back.

Shiva was pleased. He attached the head to Ganesha's body, restoring his life, and accepted the boy as his own. Thus, Ganesha and Karthikeya became brothers.[7]

Ganesha was now devoted to both his parents. One day, Shiva and Parvati called their two sons and said, 'Let's have a friendly contest. We will give the fruit of knowledge to whoever goes around the world in the least amount of time.'

Karthikeya instantly mounted his peacock and began his journey around the world. Ganesha, on the other hand, did not hurry at all. He simply walked around his parents and then bowed before them.

Parvati said affectionately, 'My dear child, what are you doing? Your brother must be halfway across the world by now—you will surely lose this race!'

Ganesha smiled at his parents with such warmth that it touched Parvati's heart. 'It does not matter, Mother. The two of you are my world and I have already encircled you. My journey is complete.'

Shiva and Parvati smiled and handed him the fruit.

---

[7] Every year, the birth of Ganesha is celebrated on the fourth day of the Hindu month of Bhadrapada

'You are such a smart child, Ganesha,' said Shiva. 'You will always have my blessing. From this day on, you will be known as the god of knowledge.'

The Mighty Mouse

Krauncha was a celestial musician in Indra's court. One day, he was running late for a performance and was walking rather hurriedly. Unfortunately, in his haste, he stepped on an old sage's foot. The sage, whose name was Vamadeva, cursed Krauncha in a fit of fury and pain. 'May you turn into a rodent that frantically scampers everywhere!'

Poor Krauncha was immediately transformed into a huge mountain rat.

As a rat he troubled many people, often creeping into farmers' homes and eating their carefully stored grains or entering ashrams and destroying their food. When the people had had enough of his troublemaking, they called upon Ganesha to help them.

Ganesha heard their pleas and threw his *pasha*, a noose, at the rat. But Krauncha managed to scamper away somehow.

'I know you are quick and can creep into any place you want to because of your size and agility, but I am going to tie you up with this pasha so that you can't trouble anyone,' said Ganesha, determined. Adjusting the rope, he carefully aimed it at the rat and, this time, caught him. The noose was tightened and Krauncha could not escape.

Krauncha pleaded with Ganesha, 'Lord, I understand my mistake and I will never trouble anyone again. Please allow

me to be your vehicle so that whenever you are worshipped, I will also be revered.'

'But will you be able to bear my weight?' asked the pot-bellied god in amusement.

'That will not be a problem. I will adjust my size according to yours.'

Ganesha agreed.

And that is how Krauncha the rat became Ganesha's primary vehicle, enabling him to move quickly and get rid of obstacles for his devotees.

Durva

A long, long time ago, there lived a fire-emitting asura named Analasura. Wherever he walked, fire burst forth, and Analasura took advantage of this great power, using it to torment people and cause widespread destruction. When he became uncontrollable, the people turned to Ganesha for help.

'Don't worry. I will take care of him,' said Ganesha and went looking for Analasura.

When Analasura saw Ganesha, he tried to swallow him. But Ganesha grew and grew, and kept growing until he was large enough to swallow the demon. The asura then promptly disappeared down Ganesha's throat and into his stomach. Everyone celebrated the end of Analasura.

Unfortunately, Ganesha soon began to suffer from excruciating pain. Analasura was using fire to wreak havoc inside his stomach!

Seeing his son's condition, Shiva released a serpent on Ganesha's stomach. The serpent's special powers were meant to have a cooling effect on Ganesha, but it was of no use. The pain persisted.

Then Vishnu came and placed a lotus on the stomach. Still, nothing happened.

Next, the river Ganga arrived and began flowing down Ganesha's torso. Brahma gave him the nectar of immortality and Vayu, the lord of the winds, blew cool air on Ganesha's tummy. Then it was the turn of the king of the Himalayas, who laid his icy hand on poor Ganesha's stomach.

Nothing helped. Everybody was baffled.

Sages from far and wide came with the hope of helping Ganesha. With their collective knowledge and wisdom, they pondered over the matter for a long time until they arrived at a potential solution.

The sages travelled to the Himalayas and brought back twenty-one blades of *durva*, a kind of grass. They asked Ganesha to consume them, who was only too happy to try anything that would relieve him from the ghastly pain. Once he ate the powerful durva, it killed Analasura, ending Ganesha's discomfort and misery.

From that day onwards, Ganesha loved durva grass, and people began using it as an offering to him.

The Slaying of the Asuras

A Tale of Three Cities

Taraka, the evil asura who had terrorized the world, had left behind three sons named Tarakaksha, Viryavana and Vidyunmali. Still enraged by the death of their father, they prayed to Brahma for many years in the hope of attaining immortality.

Brahma finally appeared, but he refused to give them what they wanted.

The three brothers then asked for an alternate boon. 'O Brahma, if you can't give us immortality, then please grant us the strength to build three indestructible, extraordinary cities. The fort of each city will be located in a different realm and will align once every thousand years. We will accept death only if a single arrow destroys all three forts during the alignment.'

Brahma smiled. 'So be it.'

With the help of the asura architect Maya, Taraka's sons built the three forts. Each was made of a different metal—gold, silver and iron.

Tarakaksha took ownership of the gold fort, located in the heavens; Viryavana got the silver fort, in the sky; and Vidyunmali took possession of the iron fort, located on earth. Together, the three cities came to be known as Tripura, and the three asuras were referred to as Tripurasuras.

Once the cities were complete, the asura became powerful and, as a result, arrogant. Their rule gradually became unbearable and the people turned to the gods for help.

Hearing the people's pleas, Shiva decided to intervene. He knew that the time of alignment was imminent, and all he needed was one potent arrow. So he called upon Vishwakarma, the architect of the heavens, and, explaining the problem, asked him, 'Will you make a special chariot and a powerful bow and arrow for me?'

Vishwakarma agreed immediately. He created a strong gold chariot with the energy of the sun, two bows named Pinaka and Sharanga and one arrow guaranteed to destroy any target. Vishwakarma gave the chariot, Pinaka and the arrow to Shiva while he presented Sharanga to Vishnu.

Armed and ready, Shiva requested Brahma to be the charioteer, and together, they sped to Tripura. The time of alignment was upon them.

With the formidable arrow, Shiva easily destroyed the three cities the moment they came together, along with the three asuras who resided in the forts.[8]

---

[8] A sculpture of this battle can be seen at Ramappa Temple in Telangana, and paintings of the event are on the ceiling of Virupaksha Temple in Hampi.

The world congratulated Shiva on a job well done. Shiva earned the title of Pinaki while Vishnu gained the moniker Sharangadeva. People decorated their homes with lights to signify the defeat of evil, a tradition that is followed even today. Lamps are lit every day after Diwali, in the Hindu month of Karthik.

Much later, Shiva decided to give the bow Pinaka to Nimi, one of his great devotees. King Nimi preserved the bow with reverence and named it Shivadhanush, or 'the bow of Shiva'. Generations went by and King Janaka was born in the same lineage. The bow's uniqueness inspired Janaka to declare that his beautiful daughter Sita would marry the man who could pick up Shivadhanush. That man turned out to be none other than Rama, of course!

The Elephant Demon

The asura Mahishasura had a son who was named Gajasura because he had the strength of multiple elephants and could use his weapon, Gajastra, to shoot arrows that transformed into elephants on the battlefield. Gajasura could not be killed by any being that held desire in its heart.

When his father died at the hands of Parvati, Gajasura became obsessed with taking revenge on all the gods. The frightened gods asked Shiva for help. Shiva, who did not desire anything, consoled them and said, 'Don't worry, my children. I will defeat him.'

Shiva and Karthikeya, commander of the heavenly army, prepared for war.

When Gajasura heard about this, he sat with his advisers to figure out a way to defeat Shiva and protect himself. Finally he realized that if he prayed to Ganesha before the war, the latter would be compelled to help him. So with great devotion, Gajasura called upon Ganesha for a blessing that would ensure his victory.

Ganesha soon appeared in front of him and said, 'My father has decided to defeat you and no one can protect you from death. I can help you in only one way. The moment his arrow touches your body, all your ignorance will disappear and you will realize eternal knowledge within yourself. I cannot stop your downfall, Gajasura, but I promise you this boon. Rest assured that you will die secure in your knowledge of the lord.'

The battle between Gajasura and Shiva began. It was a fierce clash and Gajasura was forced to use all his different weapons. When he used the varuna *astra*, the water weapon, on Shiva's head, River Ganga—residing in the lord's hair—flowed down to wash the god's feet. When Gajasura used the agni astra, the fire weapon, Ganga doused the flames. Even the *shool* astra, the axe, met its match in Shiva's trishul and was reduced to ashes. The trident, on the other hand, remained unharmed. Vayu disseminated the ashes everywhere.

As a last resort, Gajasura used the Gajastra. Thousands of elephants appeared on the battlefield, but the moment they saw Ganesha with Shiva, they bowed to him and surrendered willingly.

Now Shiva decided that it was time to end the fight. He used the varuna astra, and it pierced Gajasura's body as he closed his eyes. When he opened them again, he saw

Shiva in his actual form—not as his enemy but as his true and only god. He saw his beautiful blue skin, the crescent moon adorning his head and the goddess Ganga in his hair. Gajasura saw the *rudraksh* (Shiva's prayer-bead necklace), the third eye in the middle of his forehead, the trishul in one hand and the *damru* in the other. He saw Parvati standing next to Shiva, smiling at him. Gajasura finally realized that he had made a grave mistake, but he was glad he could see the god so clearly before he died. He knew that his end was near and began chanting the Panchakshari mantra, 'Om Namah Shivaya', over and over.

Shiva approached him and said, 'Gajasura, I had no choice but to kill you. Is there something you desire?'

'Now that I see the truth, I am happy to die by your hands. I wish to pass in the form of an elephant, and I entreat you to use my elephant skin as a part of your body after I am gone. Then I can be with you forever.'

Shiva smiled and agreed.

This is why sometimes Shiva wears the skin of an elephant.

The great battle with Gajasura, during which Ganga came down from Shiva's head and washed his feet, was fought in Kashi. Thus Kashi became famous and Shiva earned the names Vishwanatha and Gangadhara.

A Lesson to the Tigers

Dundubhi and Souhardya were cousins of the two powerful asura brothers Hiranyaksha and Hiranyakashipu. They were shape-shifters—they had the power to transform into any animal at will.

When Hiranyaksha and Hiranyakashipu were slain by the avatars of Vishnu for the havoc that they had wreaked in the world, Dundubhi and Souhardya swore to take revenge by targeting the god's followers. After careful planning, they figured out the most efficient way to stop all yagnas and holy rituals. All they needed to do was kill the priests and learned men who performed the yagnas.

The brothers went on a rampage, brutally slaughtering many priests. The people prayed to Shiva for protection.

Now it so happened that Shivratri was just around the corner. Dundubhi and Souhardya were aware that thousands of devotees would gather at Vishwanatha Temple in Kashi to worship Shiva in the form of a *shivalinga*. This was a great opportunity to slay many devotees at once and upset the gods.

On the night of the ceremony, the two asuras marched to where the Shivratri celebrations were taking place, along with a large army behind them. Using their powers to transform into tigers, they attacked everyone in the temple. People screamed out in fear. Shiva, who had been watching the events unfold, had no choice but to emerge from the shivalinga and kill the two asuras and their army instantly.

Shiva wanted to comfort his devotees and remind them that he would always guard them against any kind of assault. Thus, he decided to use tiger skin whenever he could to make sure that the slaying of Dundubhi and Souhardya would never be forgotten. This is why Shiva is often seen seated on a tiger skin.

It is believed that some lingas once had a bright light, or *jyoti*, around them because Shiva had emerged from those lingas to protect his devotees. These came to be known as jyotirlingas and are considered to be extremely sacred. There are twelve of them in India, and a person is thought to be truly blessed if they are able to visit all of them in a lifetime.

The Half-Man, Half-Woman

Sage Bhringi was a great devotee of Lord Shiva. In fact, he did not pray to anyone but the blue-necked god, who wanted the sage to include Parvati in his worship as she was a part of him. But Bhringi would not listen.

Shiva, however, did not give up. One day, he said to Bhringi, 'My beloved devotee, I'd like you to circumambulate me three times. It will bring you good fortune.'

So Bhringi transformed himself into a honeybee and flew around the lord once.

Shiva, of course, knew that Bhringi had taken the form of a bee, so he asked Parvati to sit on his lap. This way, the sage would be forced to go around Parvati as well, thus worshipping her. But to his surprise, Bhringi somehow managed to find a tiny gap between Shiva and Parvati and made sure to circle only the former on his second circuit.

Amused, Shiva made another attempt, merging his body with Parvati's—one vertical half of the body was Shiva's and the other half was Parvati's. Bhringi, though, realized what the lord had done, and so he went around half of Shiva's body and exited through the belly button.

Parvati was completely distressed by now. She cried out, 'Foolish Bhringi, you don't understand, do you? Shiva and I are like father and mother to the world. We are more important together than individually. Isn't it vital for our children to have both parents? A child gets his nerves and skeleton from the father, while the blood and flesh come from the mother. Shiva and I are inseparable. Worshipping only Shiva or me individually is nothing but incomplete reverence. As you have degraded the role of the mother, from now on you will only have your nerves and your skeleton; your blood and flesh will disappear. Your appearance will be so ugly and horrifying that people will always remember how you chose one between the mother and the father.'

The sage realized his mistake and asked for forgiveness. In time Parvati forgave him, and Bhringi became a guard at Shiva's abode along with Nandi.

This incident inspired the worship of Shiva as Ardhanarishvara, the form of half-man and-half woman. Sculptures of this form can be seen in many places in India; it is particularly well depicted in cave two of the Badami Caves in Karnataka.

The Gift of Life

Sage Mrikandu and his wife, Marudmati, were faithful devotees of Lord Shiva. One day, they prayed to him earnestly until he appeared.

Shiva asked the couple, 'What do you desire?'

'We want a child,' they replied in unison.

Shiva thought for a moment and said, 'I will give you a choice—you can either have a son who is extraordinary but will only live till the age of sixteen or a son who will live a long life but will always be a burden to you.'

The couple considered the choice carefully and said, 'We'd rather have a good son for a short duration than a bad one who will stay with us forever.'

Shiva smiled, blessed them and vanished.

Mrikandu and Marudmati soon had a beautiful child, whom they named Markandeya. He was a good son, a wonderful student and a compassionate boy. He grew up to be a great devotee of Shiva.

As the days and years rolled past, Mrikandu and Marudmati grew more and more depressed. Every now and then, they would curse the moment they had made that fateful choice. 'Maybe we should not have asked for a child at all. Having a son like Markandeya and losing him will be too painful,' they would say to each other sadly.

Markandeya was aware of his impending death, yet he continued to live his life in the best way possible and remained devoted to Shiva.

On the morning of Markandeya's sixteenth birthday, Mrikandu and Marudmati clung to their son and cried bitterly. Markandeya looked at them with love and said gently, 'I could not have had better parents than you. I have been fortunate to be born in your home.'

Bidding his sorrowful parents goodbye, Markandeya headed to Shiva's temple. He embraced the shivalinga and began chanting the Panchakshari mantra.

As the time of death was fast approaching, Yama sent his assistants to fetch the young lad. When they reached the temple, they found Markandeya lost in meditation, his arms around the shivalinga. Fearing Shiva's wrath, the assistants did not dare disturb the boy and went back.

Yama decided to perform the task himself. He went charging to the boy on his black buffalo and threw a noose around his neck. The rope, however, landed on the shivalinga instead.

A furious Shiva appeared in front of Yama, ready to fight. 'How dare you put a noose around me?' he thundered.

Yama hung his head in surrender.

Shiva offered to let the matter go but only if Yama returned without claiming Markandeya.

The god of death agreed and Markandeya's life was spared, much to the joy of his parents.

Markandeya's story represents the belief that the Shiva Panchakshari mantra can turn the tide.

This incident is said to have happened in the temple town of Thirukkadaiyur in the state of Tamil Nadu.

Markandeya eventually resided in a place now known as Markandeya Tirtha, which is on the way to Yamunotri, the source of River Yamuna. He is said to have written the Markandeya Purana there, one of the eighteen major Puranas.

The Innocent Hunter

Kannappa was an orphan boy, who had been brought up by a gang of hunters in the forest. He had no formal education— the only thing he knew was how to survive, hunting and eating his kill and sustaining himself on fruits from the forest and water from the river.

One day, he lost his way and chanced upon a stone structure on a riverbed. People were walking in and out of it, carrying flowers, fruits and coconuts. The structure was a temple, but Kannappa had never seen one before and so was curious to know more about it.

He waited until almost everyone had left for the day. Finally he saw a young boy coming out of the stone building and decided to speak to him.

Kannappa asked him many questions in his crude language. 'What is this building called? Why are people bringing things with them and leaving them inside?'

The boy was surprised at his ignorance and baffled by his questions, but still tried his best to answer them. 'This is the temple of Lord Shiva. People come here to offer fruits and flowers to him. They ask Shiva for whatever they desire and Shiva listens to all their prayers.'

Kannappa immediately wanted to visit the temple. The boy showed him the way inside and told him about the shivalinga.

Kannappa asked the boy innocently, 'This shivalinga . . . does it give us whatever we ask for?'

'Yes, that's what we believe,' he said. 'It is getting dark now—I must get home.' And he went away, leaving Kannappa alone.

Hesitantly, Kannappa entered the temple. He sat down in a corner and wondered how a stone could give anyone what they wished for. So he decided to test it.

'O Shiva, please let me hunt enough prey so that I do not remain hungry. I don't have any fruits or flowers to offer you. But if you give me the prey, I will share it with you. I promise I will not cheat you,' he declared.

The next morning, Kannappa went hunting. He searched for prey all day but did not find any. Hungry and frustrated by late afternoon, he was sure that the boy at the temple had lied to him. Still, he continued the hunt. Just as evening fell, he spotted two rabbits coming out of their burrows and killed them. Since he had promised the lord that he would share his prey, he went to the temple with one of the dead rabbits.

It was late and the temple was deserted. Kannappa entered and said out loud, 'Please come and take your share, my lord. This is for you.'

He sat and waited till it was dark but the lord did not appear. Kannappa began feeling hungry and sleepy, and decided to leave the rabbit in the temple. He entreated Shiva to take the promised share once more before heading home.

When people came to the temple the next morning, they found the dead rabbit in front of the shivalinga. The devotees were very upset. 'Who has brought this here? How dare they desecrate our temple?'

The dead rabbit was thrown out.

The next day, Kannappa went to hunt for his meal again, but this time he had no luck. He thought, 'I should go to the temple tonight and ask Shiva how he enjoyed his rabbit meal.'

To his surprise, there were hordes of people at the temple that night. It was the night of Shivratri, but how was the orphan hunter boy to know that?

Kannappa looked around and noticed the young boy he had spoken to praying to Shiva inside the temple. Since he was not used to being around so many people, he decided to wait and climbed a bael tree nearby. It was a long wait and, having nothing better to do, he started plucking the leaves off the tree and throwing them to the ground. Unknown to him, there was a small shivalinga under the tree, which had not been worshipped for a long time. The bael leaves fell on this shivalinga.

Meanwhile, the Shivratri festivities inside the temple continued. People sang bhajans and worshipped the lord with flowers and fruits.

Kannappa was enchanted by the bhajans, and slowly started singing along and chanting the Panchakshari mantra.

The night turned into early morning and the devotees departed from the temple. Kannappa climbed down from the tree and entered the inner sanctum.

He saw that Shiva's eyes, on the shivalinga, had red marks on them. They were probably just from the kumkum or the small red flowers that the people had offered, but Kannappa was sure that Shiva was having trouble with his eyes. He felt sad for what he perceived as Shiva's sorry state and wanted to help him. 'Poor Shiva!' he thought. 'He lives here all alone and has no one to take care of him when he is sick. He doesn't even get a meal until the devotees visit him.'

Kannappa had seen the devotees pouring water on the shivalinga the night before. 'The lord must be feeling cold. Perhaps he is shivering,' he thought. 'After all, he is only covered with leaves!'

So he asked Shiva, 'What can I get you, my lord? Maybe some food or medicine? How can I serve you?'

Shiva did not answer him.

'Oh, no!' thought Kannappa. 'The lord must indeed be very, very ill, for he is unable to reply!'

Immediately, he went to the forest, fetched some medicinal herbs and applied their paste on the red marks. But nothing happened.

'Oh, no! I think he has gone blind! I must give the lord one of my eyes to help him get better. That will surely make him happy!' exclaimed Kannappa, his heart pure and true.

He picked up the trident and pointed it towards his right eye, balancing one leg on the shivalinga and the other on the ground.

The boy was illiterate, had no knowledge of mantras or of the proper ways of worship, but his devotion knew no bounds. Just as he was about to pierce his own eye, Shiva appeared with his consort, Parvati. Unknowingly Kannappa had fasted on Shivratri, worshipped the lord with bael leaves and proved that his heart was untainted. And so Shiva was pleased.

'You have won me over with your innocence,' said the lord, smiling. 'People promise me things all the time but they forget to keep their word the moment they get what they want. You, on the other hand, treated me like a fellow human being, and that is very rare indeed. From now on, you will be considered my greatest devotee and your name will forever be associated with mine. May you live for many, many years.'

The temple is still around, in the town of Srikalahasti in Andhra Pradesh.

The Girl That God Took

A long, long time ago, there lived a rich man in a small village named Koluru in Karnataka. He was a great devotee of Lord Shiva and would visit the temple every morning with a tumbler of milk as offering. His wife passed away early and he only had a daughter—a sweet, good-natured girl named Kodagusu.

Every morning at the temple, the man would chant the Shiva Panchakshari mantra five times. Then he would drink the milk he had brought with him and take the empty tumbler home. Kodagusu would greet her father at the door, take the tumbler and wash it so that it would be clean and ready for her father the next day. This routine continued for several years.

One day, the man had to travel to another village for work. He said to Kodagusu, 'My dear daughter, for years I have made an offering to the lord every day. Shiva has always protected and helped us, and I don't want to upset him. So make sure you go to the temple tomorrow on my behalf and offer the lord a tumbler of milk.'

Kodagusu agreed, and her father left in peace.

The next morning, Kodagusu took a bath, combed her hair and put on a pretty dress. She heated a little milk, adding sugar, poured it into the tumbler and carefully carried it to the temple. She garlanded the shivalinga and placed the milk in front of the deity.

'O Shiva,' she said, 'my father, who is a great devotee of yours, has asked me to bring this milk to you. Please accept this offering and drink it.'

She sat for some time in a corner of the room, waiting for Shiva to turn up for the milk, but nobody appeared and the tumbler of milk remained full.

'Maybe Shiva has not heard my request,' she thought and repeated aloud, 'I am Kodagusu, daughter of your beloved follower who offers you milk every day. Please drink it as soon as possible because I have to go home quickly and leave for school.'

She waited for another five minutes, but there was still no sign of Shiva. 'Perhaps he's feeling shy because my face is unfamiliar. I'll give him some privacy,' she thought, and went out.

Kodagusu waited outside for some time and then went back in to check if the offering had been accepted. The milk was still untouched.

Now she started to worry. 'If Shiva does not drink the milk and I take it back, my father will scold me. Why isn't the lord listening to me?' she wondered.

She sat in front of the shivalinga and cajoled the lord, 'Please drink the milk. You need it to remain strong. I even added some sugar today so it tastes quite sweet. I'm sure that you will like it. Please don't get me into trouble—have the milk! If you drink it today, I will bring you laddoos tomorrow.'

She heard nothing but silence.

Helpless, Kodagusu began crying. Time ticked by and morning turned to noon. Shiva remained where he was and Kodagusu filled the air with her occasional bouts of sobbing. She was scared of her father and tired of the obstinate god. Overcome by frustration, she started hitting her head against the shivalinga. 'Lord, am I doing something wrong? What am I supposed to tell my father if you don't accept our offering?'

Her pleas reached Shiva's ears on Mount Kailash. His heart was moved by her innocence and he emerged from the shivalinga.

Kodagusu was ecstatic to see him. She smiled brightly and exclaimed, 'You look very different from your pictures—so kind and so . . . normal. Tell me, why were you hiding for so long?'

Without waiting for a response, she continued, 'Well, never mind that now. I am glad you are here. Please drink this quickly and give the tumbler back to me.'

Shiva promptly drank the milk and handed her the empty tumbler. Kodagusu thanked him and ran all the way home. The god watched her for some time with affection and then went back to his abode.

After reaching home, Kodagusu washed the tumbler, grabbed her bag and hurried to attend the remainder of her school day.

In the evening, her father came back from his journey tired but happy. The trip had been fruitful and he had made a good business deal. While resting, he thought, 'Shiva is great! I had a good day thanks to his blessings. Perhaps I will offer him some laddoos tomorrow as a show of my gratitude.'

At that moment, he remembered the task he had assigned to his daughter and turned to her. 'Kodagusu, did you take some milk for the lord today?'

'Yes, I did, but Shiva took hours and hours to come! I had to cajole and plead and scold him until he finally drank the milk! Father, you don't take so much time when you go to the temple. Maybe Shiva listens to you easily because you are older than I am and he knows you. Maybe I am just too young and it takes a long time for him to hear my request.'

Kodagusu's father was taken aback. 'Child, come here and sit down,' he said. 'Tell me again what you just said, but slowly.'

Kodagusu narrated the incident in detail.

The man could not believe it. He knew that his daughter never lied, but how could Shiva really emerge from the shivalinga? He thought, 'Was there someone in the temple who looked like Shiva and fooled my young daughter into giving him the milk? The poor thing! She has most definitely been duped. Let me ask her to take the milk to the lord tomorrow and follow her to see what happens.'

The man did not sleep well that night.

The next morning, he said to his daughter, 'Here, take this milk and go offer it to the lord in the temple.'

'Father, please come with me. I will show you how long he takes to appear. He'll make me late for school again!'

'No, Kodagusu, off you go to the temple now. I will go some other day,' he said.

The girl nodded obediently and left with the milk.

Quietly, her father followed her to the temple, stood behind the door and peeped in. Just like the day before, Kodagusu greeted the lord and asked him to drink the milk, but no one appeared. She pleaded for some time but to no avail.

Kodagusu looked around the temple—it was completely deserted. By now her father was convinced that some passer-by had indeed seized the opportunity to pose as Shiva and drink the milk. Upset, he came out from behind the door and scolded his daughter, 'Shiva did not come here yesterday! It was someone pretending to be him. You, my little girl, fell for his antics like a big fool!'

'No, it *was* Shiva,' said Kodagusu earnestly. 'I am absolutely certain. His neck was blue and he had long curly hair. There was a half-moon on his head and he was holding a trident. When he smiled at me, I noticed the rudraksh necklace around his neck. I gave him the milk, Father. He *is* real. I am not lying!'

But her father refused to believe her.

Kodagusu was heartbroken by his lack of faith in her. She hugged the linga desperately and called out to Shiva. 'O lord, please come and reveal yourself. If you don't, my father will think I am a liar. You are the only one who can prove the truth to him. I don't deserve to be scolded for a lie that I haven't told.'

Suddenly, there was a thunderous noise and the shivalinga opened. Shiva emerged from it and embraced Kodagusu. Then he looked at her father and said, 'Children are innocent. I don't want anyone to test her again or compel me to come here when she calls out to me. She will stay with me forever.'

Shiva held on to Kodagusu as the linga began to close. He obviously intended to take her with him.

Kodagusu's shocked father ran to the linga but only managed to grab a few strands of her hair before it shut completely.

Legend has it that this is why when a person touches the shivalinga in Koluru village, they feel like they are stroking someone's hair.

The Story of Adi Shankara

Kaladi is a village located to the east of River Periyar in the Ernakulum district of Kerala. In the early eighth century, a young widow named Areyamba lived there with her son, Shankara.

Young Shankara was a keen observer of life and the events that happened around him. He was exceptionally intelligent and had taken to the idea of becoming an ascetic since he was a child. He would ask his mother every now and then, 'Will you allow me to become a hermit?'

Areyamba was afraid of losing her only son and vehemently disapproved of the notion.

Shankara did not want to displease his mother, so he remained quiet. But he did not give up hope.

One day, when he was eight years old, a crocodile grabbed his foot and bit into it savagely while he was bathing in the river. His mother screamed for help but there was no one around.

'Amma!' cried out Shankara. 'If you give me permission to become a sage, the crocodile will let go of my foot. Don't ask me how I know—I just do!'

His mother sobbed, completely helpless.

'Please, Amma. Say something. Will you let me follow the path my heart desires?'

Areyamba wanted to save her son at any cost and so she nodded.

Immediately the crocodile opened its jaws and swam away.

Days later, as Shankara was about to depart from his mother's home in search of truth, Areyamba extracted a promise from him. 'No matter where you are, my son, you must come back when you hear of my death to perform my last rites,' she said.

Shankara soon became the disciple of Guru Govindapada. The young prodigy studied the Vedas, the Upanishads, the Brahmasutra and many more texts. He travelled all over India and spread the philosophy of Advaita,[9] for which he

---

[9] It is a philosophy that preaches that the soul and God are one.

is remembered even today. He established many *mathas* or monasteries, of which four are still famous. The first was Sringeri in Karnataka, where he established the Saraswati temple. The other mathas are in Kedar, Puri and Dwarka. Shankara also had many illustrious disciples, such as Sureshvara, Prithvidhara, Bodhendra and Brahmendra. He is believed to be an avatar of Shiva. Eventually, he settled down in the ancient village of Maheswati in Mithila, which is now in Bihar, where he wrote several important books that are still read today.

Shankara was known to frequently defeat the most learned scholars in debates with his logic and the skillful expression of his extraordinary thoughts and beliefs. Once, in a debate, he was pitted against the celebrated philosopher Mandana Misra. The referee was to be Mandana Misra's wife, Ubhaya Bharati, who was known for her impartiality. Both husband and wife were famous for their knowledge and understanding of Indian philosophy. The agreement was that if Mandana Misra lost, he would live the life of a hermit; and if Shankara lost, he would marry and live the life of a householder.

The debate went on for days until, finally, Shankara won. The win was especially hard for Ubhaya Bharati as it affected her life as well. However, she remained objective and pronounced the verdict in Shankara's favour.

Following the decision, Mandana Misra took on the name of Sureshvara and became Shankara's follower. He was supposedly one of the first acharyas of the matha in Sringeri.

At the age of thirty-two, though, Shankara suddenly disappeared from Kedarnath, never to be heard of again.

However, his legacy remains intact even today, and he is still considered to be one of the brightest minds in Indian history.

The King of Kerala

A long time ago, there lived a pious king in Kerala, who was a great devotee of the goddess Bhagavati. He ruled his kingdom justly, and his subjects adored him. He would frequently disguise himself as a common man and wander around to observe and talk to people about the true state of the kingdom.

One day, while returning to the palace after one of his visits, he passed Bhagavati's temple. It was the middle of the night and the premises were deserted. There, he saw a well-dressed lady with long hair sitting in the temple veranda, crying. Seeing how late it was, he was surprised to find her alone.

He approached her. 'Mother, I see that you are crying. Please tell me what is bothering you. Perhaps I can help.'

Wiping her tears, the lady said, 'Oh my dear child, I am truly in distress for I have to leave this place forever.'

'Why?'

'I am the Rajalakshmi of this kingdom. I bring prosperity and peace, along with wealth. But my time here is over and I must leave.'

'But what has changed? Why must you leave?' asked the king.

'Life is filled with ups and downs, and this kingdom's downfall begins tomorrow. I don't want to leave, but I must.'

'Is there anything I can do?' the king asked, still not revealing his identity. He was rather concerned by the lady's mysterious words.

'Only the people of this land can help—they must somehow make me stay here.'

The king was quiet for a minute. 'All right, let me think about this. In the meantime, I want to go inside the temple and pray to the goddess to show us the way. But first, I must have a bath. Kind lady, will you please do me a favour and hold my clothes for me until I come back from the stepwell?'

The lady nodded. 'Come back quickly. Dawn is near and I don't have much time left,' she said sadly.

'Will you promise to wait till I return?'

'I promise, and I always keep my word. Just come back as soon as you can,' she replied.

The king went to the stepwell on the temple grounds. He turned back to look at the lady holding his clothes and prayed to the goddess, 'O devi, it doesn't matter if I lose my life, but I can't let you leave this kingdom and watch my subjects fall into despair. My people must always be prosperous, and it is my duty to see that they never suffer.'

Then the selfless king entered the stepwell and drowned himself in the water.

The lady waited and waited. When it was morning, she realized that he would never come back. Since she had given her word that she would wait for him, she quietly went back inside the temple.

And that is how the king took care of his subjects and the goddess of wealth remained in the state of Kerala.

Sambhavami Yuge Yuge

The Bones of Dadhichi

Dadhichi was a pious and kind sage, and an ardent devotee of Lord Vishnu. He was the author of the famous Narayana Kavacham *stotra*.

Whenever the devas lost to the asuras in battle, they would leave their weapons with Dadhichi, who stood guard over them.

Once, the devas did not come for their arms for a long, long time because there was no war. Decades went by, and Dadhichi got bored of taking care of the munitions. He knew a special mantra called Madhuvidya, by which he used to transform the weapons into liquid. He would then immerse that in water and drink the solution. That way he was free to travel around and carry the arms with him.

Meanwhile, a mighty asura named Vritrasura had obtained a rather dangerous boon from Lord Brahma. No weapon made of either wood or metal could kill him. His immunity to weapons made him even more powerful and, as a result, Vritrasura became arrogant and malevolent.

One day, he stole all the water in the world. Men, women and children began to die of thirst everywhere.

Their desperate prayers and cries for help eventually reached Indra, the king of the devas, who immediately went to Sage Dadhichi to reclaim the divine weapons.

Since the weapons were nowhere in sight, Indra shouted at Dadhichi, 'What have you done with all our arms? Did you lose them? How could you be so irresponsible?'

Dadhichi listened patiently as Indra raged about Vritrasura and the boon that had made him unbeatable.

Finally he smiled and said, 'I have all the weapons you need. I used my powers to dissolve the weapons in water, which I drank. But don't worry. I will leave my body—the devas can use my bones to create weapons made of neither wood nor metal. Your victory is certain.'

Ashamed of his outburst, Indra hastily apologized to Dadhichi, while wondering if there was a way to save the sage somehow.

'This body is not permanent, my lord,' the sage said. 'I have to die some day. You must let me do it now, when I can be of assistance to the gods.'

Indra nodded sadly.

Dadhichi then left his physical form through his yogic powers as well as blessings from the lord. Indra created a weapon named Vajrayudha from the sage's spine and other arms from the remaining bones. The weapon Vajrayudha was as hard as a diamond, and Indra used it to defeat Vritrasura.

Finally, water was restored to the earth, thanks to Dadhichi's noble sacrifice, and the people celebrated with much joy and relief.

The Churning of the Ocean

One day, the short-tempered sage Durvasa happened to meet a celestial nymph named Sumati, who was carrying a lotus garland giving off a heady fragrance. Enchanted by the smell, Durvasa immediately wanted it for himself. So he asked Sumati, 'Please may I have that garland?'

Sumati did not want to part with it, but she was afraid of the sage's unpredictable temper and gave it to him reluctantly.

Durvasa enjoyed the fragrance of the garland for a while and then decided that he would offer it to Indra. Indra was proud of his handsome looks, his station and his gorgeous wife, Shachi.

However, to Durvasa's disappointment, Indra didn't seem to care for the gift at all. He just accepted it and immediately placed it on the trunk of his favourite elephant. The elephant, unable to stand the strong aroma for too long, threw the garland to the ground and stomped on it.

Predictably, Durvasa lost his temper and cursed Indra. 'The power that comes with being the king of the gods has obviously gone to your head. You have lost the ability to graciously receive a gift. I curse you as well as your subjects because they have failed to stand up to you and inform you of your shortcomings. You will all soon lose your strength and become a weak reflection of your old selves.'

The curse came to fruition and the devas began losing all their battles against the asuras. At the time, the king of asuras was Bali, grandson of the famous Prahlada, and he had control over almost the entire earth.

Overcome by despair, the devas approached Vishnu.

'You need to learn some diplomacy,' he said with a mysterious smile. Then he added, 'There is a pot of nectar at the bottom of the ocean. Churn the ocean, and the pot is yours. One sip is enough to make you immortal. Be warned that Bali is also aware of its existence, and the ocean can only be churned with the combined strength of the devas and the asuras. Now it is up to you to accomplish this, and I will, of course, be there to guide you.'

Happy that there was a solution in sight, Indra approached Bali and somehow convinced both sides to join forces for this one task.

Using Mount Mandara as a churning rod and Vasuki, the king of serpents, as the rope, the churning began. The asuras chose the end with Vasuki's head, which they assumed was stronger, while the devas decided to follow Vishnu's advice and stay towards the serpent's tail. Vishnu knew that Vasuki's mouth would emit poisonous fumes during the process of churning and did not want the gods to inhale those fumes. He also knew that the asuras would be able to withstand the poison.

After some time, the rod began to sink. Vishnu immediately took the form of a turtle and balanced Mount Mandara on his back. And so the ocean continued to be stirred.

The churning released many unexpected and magical things.

The first was Lakshmi, the goddess of wealth. She emerged from a lotus, bejewelled and wearing a red sari. When she saw the handsome Vishnu in his true form, she accepted him as her husband and became his eternal consort.

Next was the Kaustubha, the most valuable jewel in the world, which Vishnu claimed.

The Kaustubha was followed by the fragrant divine flowering tree, Parijat, that Indra was happy to plant in his royal garden.

The asuras, however, ignored all these things and focused only on getting the nectar.

But there was more to come.

The moon god Chandra emerged and adorned Shiva's head.

Chandra was quickly followed by the deadly poison Halahala. At this, the asuras and devas panicked. If even one drop of the poison fell on earth, it would ignite and burst into flames, destroying everyone. When nobody offered to take the responsibility of handling the Halahala, Shiva decided to take matters into his own hands. He drank the venom before Parvati could stop him. The goddess frantically grasped his neck to avoid the poison from going further down his body. As a result, Shiva's neck turned blue and has remained so ever since. This is how he earned the name Neelkanth, or 'the lord with the blue throat', and Najunda, or 'the lord who has consumed poison'.

Then came the Ashwini Kumars, the divine physicians. As the devas wanted them, the twins went to Devaloka.

Next was Kamadhenu, the divine cow that could fulfil all the desires of her owner. Vishnu granted her to the sages who performed penance for him.

She was followed by a stunning white elephant with five trunks, named Airavata, who became Indra's primary vehicle. And he was followed by the seven-headed horse called Uchaishravas. Then the apsaras, the ethereal dancing maidens, emerged, whom Indra wanted in his court.

At last, the moment everyone had been waiting for arrived—the pot of immortality in the form of sweet nectar surged out of the ocean of milk.

Vishnu knew that the asuras would not give up the pot and that if they drank it, it would unleash hell on earth. So he took the form of a striking maiden named Mohini and began to distract the asuras.

'Oh, you poor asuras!' said Mohini. 'All of you have suffered from Vasuki's toxic fumes. Why don't you have a bath and wash yourselves? I will serve you this precious nectar myself then.'

The asuras, hypnotized by Mohini's words and beauty, did as she said and scurried away to the nearest river.

Seizing the opportunity, Mohini started ladling out the nectar to the devas.

What Vishnu didn't know was that there were two asuras, Rahu and Ketu, who had been wary of Mohini's charm and had not left the place. They sat amidst the devas silently and in disguise, waiting for the nectar. It was only after Vishnu had given them the nectar that he realized who they were. Without waiting for a single moment, he beheaded them with his divine discus. But because their mouths were already filled with nectar, they survived.

Meanwhile, Vishnu asked his vehicle, Garuda, to transport the remaining nectar to Devaloka.

When the asuras came back after their bath to drink the nectar, there was no sight of Mohini, the devas or the nectar. Disappointed and enraged, Bali vowed to take revenge when the time was right.

Legend has it that the birth of Vishnu's turtle avatar (called Kurma) took place at Sri Kurma Temple near Srikakulam, in Andhra Pradesh.

The Kaustubha jewel can be seen today at Venkateshwara Temple in Tirupati, where the jewel is located on the deity's shoulder.

Rahu and Ketu are worshipped as planets today.

When Garuda was carrying the nectar to Devaloka, a few drops fell to the earth and today that place is home to Garuda's temple, named Vainateya, located in the state of Andhra Pradesh.

It is believed that a drop each from the pot (or *kumbh*) containing nectar fell in four spots: in present-day Haridwar, which is on the banks of River Ganga; in Prayag Raj (present-day Allahabad), which is at the confluence of the rivers Ganga, Yamuna and Saraswati; in Nasik, on the banks of River Godavari; and in Ujjain, on the banks of River Kshipra. At each of these four places, the Kumbh Mela is celebrated once in twelve years, and legend goes that whoever takes a dip in the river at this time will be absolved of their sins.

The story about the churning of the ocean remains popular with artists all over India and is frequently depicted in various forms and styles. Carvings of this can be seen along the walls of the Angkor Wat temple complex in Cambodia, while a statue of Vishnu in the form of Mohini can be found at Shri Mahalasa Temple of Goa.

The Ten Avatars

Mother Earth, who was also known as Bhu Devi, once came to Vaikuntha seeking Vishnu. She seemed to be greatly upset about something and was in tears.

Vishnu tried to console her. 'Bhu Devi, why are you so unhappy? You are the one responsible for the survival of all animals, plants and the human race. You have endless patience and kindness in your heart. People walk all over you, but still you smile and give them food, shelter and clothing. You are such a great mother. It pains me to see you like this. Tell me, what is troubling you so much?'

'My lord,' sobbed Bhu Devi. 'My burden has multiplied—there are far more evil people in the world than the good ones. These people are constantly lying, cheating, killing animals or harassing everybody around, including women and children. Their greed has no end. To make things worse, sometimes they even get boons from Brahma or Shiva. If this anarchy continues, a day will come when I won't be able to bear it any more and the world will end. Will you help me?'

Vishnu smiled. 'Yes, Bhu Devi. I understand what you are saying, but I promise you, whenever the bad outweighs the good, I will come to earth in an avatar and protect all that is good in the world.'

'How many avatars will there be, my lord?'

'Ten,' said Vishnu. 'They will be called the *dashavatars*. I will always be born as a mortal and die as one too, and my consort, Lakshmi, will be born as my wife on some of these visits. I will kill great asuras and fight many wars in these forms.'

'What kind of avatars will they be?'

'The first will be the Matsya avatar, in which I will be born as a fish and protect the earth at the time of the *jalapralaya*, when the earth will be struck by a great flood. The second will be the turtle Kurma and I will play my role during the churning of the ocean. Third, I will come as the wild boar Varaha to slay the great asura Hiranyaksha and protect the earth. In the fourth avatar, I will come as the half-lion and half-man Narasimha to kill Hiranyakashipu. Then I will appear as the learned dwarf Vamana in my fifth avatar and defeat the mighty Bali.'

Bhu Devi listened carefully, as if she was memorizing every word.

'The sixth one will be Parashurama, and I will punish the powerful and mighty rulers for their thoughtless actions and their horrendous mistakes,' continued Vishnu. 'In the seventh avatar, I will kill King Ravana in my form as Rama. The eighth avatar will be Krishna, through whom I will kill Dantavakra, assassinate the cruel kings Kansa and Shishupala and become an integral part of the Mahabharata war. My ninth will be Buddha, the peaceful sage, who will teach the importance of following the middle path between materialism and spiritualism. In my last and final birth, I will appear as the white horse Kalki and destroy the evil in the world.'

Finally, Vishnu looked at Bhu Devi affectionately and said, 'You don't have to worry about the weight of evil in the world. Whenever you need me, I will come and reduce your burden.'

Bhu Devi bowed her head and smiled, thankful for the assistance she would be given in the times to come.

The Big Fish

The first human creation of Lord Brahma was a man named Manu. We are believed to be his descendants.

One day, when Manu was offering water to the sun god, Surya, he noticed a tiny fish in the water cupped in his palms. He took pity on the little thing, put it in his *kamandalu* and brought it home.

The next morning, Manu saw the fish peeping out from the small water pot. When he went closer, he found that the fish had grown many times its original size. So he took the fish and released it in a pond nearby.

Within a day, the fish grew to such a size that it occupied the entire pond.

Manu was surprised at the rate at which the fish was growing, but he still wanted to save it. So he transported the fish to the closest lake.

But even the lake wasn't big enough for it. Soon, the fish was placed in a river and eventually, in the sea. But it wouldn't stop growing.

Finally, Manu asked the fish, 'Who are you?'

'I am Vishnu,' replied the fish. 'I have come to warn you of an impending disaster. The world is about to be submerged in water. Gather as many seeds, plants, animals, men, women, children and sacred texts as you can, and build a boat that can carry all of it. When the flood comes, tie the boat to my fins and I will take you to a safe spot. After the water recedes, you can rebuild the world. Everyone will remember you, and you will come to be known as the father of mankind, or Manukula.'

Manu didn't quite understand the gravity of the situation but decided to obey the god anyway.

Just as the end of the world was about to begin, an asura named Hayagriva stole the Vedas. And then, as predicted, the flood hit the earth and within seven days, it was completely submerged.

Once Vishnu had transported Manu and the boat to a safe haven, he went in search of Hayagriva and killed him. He rescued the Vedas, which became a guide for the new world and the future generations.

This story appears in various mythologies and holy texts in different forms. It is similar to the story of Noah's ark, which is said to have taken place in the region of the Caspian Sea. According to an old Indian legend, the Caspian Sea is none other than the Kashyapa Samudra of the ancient world, named after the famous sage Kashyapa.

The Large Dwarf

The great asura king Bali, grandson of Prahlada, was frequently referred to as Mahabali because of his greatness.

Unlike a lot of his ancestors, he was good to his subjects and very generous.

Bali's consistently fair and just rule as well as his increasing strength worried Indra. He wondered what would happen if Bali ever decided to fight the devas and usurp his own throne. If such an event were to occur, Indra wasn't sure if he'd be able to defeat Bali.

As feared, as the decades passed, Bali changed, becoming proud and arrogant. Inevitably, his actions took a turn for the worse. So Vishnu decided that Bali must be taught a lesson that he would never forget.

It was common knowledge that Bali fulfilled the desires of anyone who asked him for a gift during the performance of his yagnas. So Vishnu took the form of a young dwarf named Vamana and approached the king during one of his yagnas.

When Bali saw the dwarf coming towards him, he stood up and offered Vamana a seat.

Vamana said, 'Emperor Bali, I have heard that you are a very generous man. So I have come to ask you for something.'

'What is it that you want, little one?' asked Bali. 'If it is in my power, I will give you whatever your heart desires.'

'My request is quite insignificant. But you have to promise to grant it.'

Bali smiled. 'I promise,' he said.

'In that case, I want three steps of land. Each step must equal the size of one of my feet,' said Vamana humbly.

Bali laughed and laughed. It took him several minutes to settle down from the hilarity of the idea—a request for such a small piece of land! 'Ask for more than that, little man. You should request for something more befitting an emperor's donation.'

Vamana bowed. 'I know that you are a generous man, but I know my limits. Please forgive me if this is too trivial for a man such as yourself.'

Bali's teacher Shukracharya, who had been observing this interaction keenly, instinctively grasped that something was out of place and that Vamana was not who he appeared to be. He called Bali and advised him, 'O my king, please don't accept Vamana's condition. Something is wrong here and it makes me uneasy. I fear that this may be a scheme by the devas who are too afraid to face you directly. As your teacher and a well-wisher, I must advise you against getting entangled in this.'

'Respected guru, I have already given my word to Vamana and hence I must fulfil it. In any case, what can this little man do to a mighty king like me?' said the king.

Saying thus, Bali turned to Vamana, who was patiently waiting behind him.

Bali's wife, who stood nearby, nodded to indicate that she was in agreement with her husband.

'May I take the first step?' asked Vamana.

'Yes,' replied Bali.

As was the custom in the olden days, the gift-giver would take some water in their right palm and drop it gently on to Mother Earth. This was a sign that the giver was donating wholeheartedly with Mother Earth as his true witness. The actual gift could only be given after this ritual was completed. Thus, a jug was brought to Bali, who cupped a little water in his palm and let it trickle on to the ground.

Vamana lifted one foot, ready to take his first step. To everyone's amazement, he no longer remained a dwarf. He grew taller and taller until the top of his head went beyond the clouds. His feet became so huge that they occupied all of the earth.

'The earth is mine,' announced Vamana and shrunk back to his original size.

Bali was aghast. He had lost all that he had conquered. His guru had been right. Vamana was not an ordinary dwarf, after all. A fleeting thought crossed Bali's mind. 'Maybe he is Vishnu?'

'O Mahabali, where should I take my second step?' asked Vamana.

'The sky, sir,' replied Bali. Again, he took water from the jug and poured some on to the earth.

Vamana grew in size again and took possession of the sky with one stride. With that, there was nothing left for the king to give.

Vamana diminished in size and looked at Bali. 'What about my third footstep?' he questioned him.

This time, Guru Shukracharya could not restrain himself any longer. He turned himself into a mosquito and entered the water jug. Quickly, he flew to the mouth of the jug and blocked the opening with his tiny body in such a way that no water would flow from the jug even when it was tilted.

King Bali, however, was ignorant of his guru's activities. He bowed his head and spoke to Vamana. 'Sir, it is clear that you are none other than Vishnu. You first appeared in the form of a boar in front of my great-granduncle, Hiranyaksha, and then visited my great-grandfather, Hiranyakashipu, and my grandfather, Prahlada, in the form of Narasimha. You assisted the churning of the ocean in the form of the turtle Kurma. Now you have blessed me with your presence as Vamana. Our family is lucky indeed that you have chosen us to be in your presence four times. May I request you to place your foot on my head as your third and final step?'

Saying thus, Bali tried to pour the water from the jug again but Shukracharya kept blocking the flow of water.

Clever Vamana picked up a thin stick and poked the water jug precisely where the mosquito was hiding. The stick pierced Shukracharya's eye, and he immediately flew out of the jug writhing in pain. Instantly, a stream began flowing from the jug, and from that day onwards, Shukracharya had to live with only one eye.

Now Vamana placed his foot on Bali's head and pushed him to Pataal, the lower realm of the world, thus removing him from earth.

Once the dust had settled, Vamana said to Bali, 'I know that you are one of the finest and kindest emperors any subject can dream of, but your arrogance is responsible for what has happened to you. Still, I am struck by your large-heartedness and your commitment to keeping your word, and so I'd like to grant you a boon. Tell me, what do you want?'

Bali smiled. 'I don't want anything grand, my lord. Your presence and teachings are a boon for me on their own. Great sages and devotees spend their lifetimes just to get a glimpse of you. I am indeed fortunate. However, if you really want to grant me something, then please let me visit my kingdom once a year to check on the welfare of my subjects. I need nothing more.'

Vishnu, surprised by Bali's simple appeal, granted him his wish. Then he said, 'O Bali, but I would like to give you a boon too. You had graciously offered your head for me to place my foot on, knowing the potential consequences. From this day on, I will be your guard in Pataal. This will show the world that I can even be a devotee's servant if his devotion is pure.'

Bali bowed in happiness.

Hence the festival of Onam is celebrated today in Kerala, as it is the day Bali comes to earth and visits his kingdom to see his people.

> This avatar of Vishnu is also known as Trivikrama because of his conquest of the three worlds with three steps. Many sculptures and paintings of this incident are found in our country, the most famous of which can be seen in cave three of the Badami Caves.

The Axeman

A long time ago, there lived a scholarly and quick-tempered sage named Jamadagni. He resided in a small home deep in a forest and lived a simple life.

Princess Renuka lived a life of luxury, in a palace in the capital city of the kingdom. Renuka was both intelligent and stunning. One day, she and her friends went to a forest, where Jamadagni was staying for a trip. As was destined, Renuka met the sage in his abode. The stark lack of grandeur was apparent in the sage's appearance and yet the sense of calm and contentment he exuded enchanted the princess. She couldn't tear her eyes away from him. When she returned to the palace, she told her father that she desired to marry Jamadagni.

Renuka's father sent word to the sage, telling him about his daughter's wish, but Jamadagni refused the proposal. He said, 'I am a hermit and I reside on the outskirts of the forest with very few comforts. My mind is busy with questions of spiritual learning. Renuka is a beautiful princess and she is used to a life of luxuries. She will be unable to adjust to my way of life.'

But Princess Renuka remained adamant. She went to meet the sage herself in order to convince him. 'I am sure that I want you to be my life partner, and I am prepared to change my way of living to suit yours,' she said.

'Renuka, I don't want you to regret your decision and long for the lost luxuries later on. That, in itself, will reflect your yearning for your earlier lifestyle, and I am afraid my temper may lead to some terrible curse that will spell your doom. I will not take such a risk. It is better that we don't marry.'

'I swear I will forget my past life completely and never even think of it once we are married,' replied the princess. She was persistent, and in time, Jamadagni gave in.

Soon, the two were wed and Renuka began to live her husband's simple, austere way of life. Later, they had many children, the eldest of whom was Parashurama. He grew up to be an obedient son devoted to his parents. His temper, however, was inherited from his father.

One day, when Renuka was fetching water from a river nearby, she saw a *gandharva* and an apsara locked in a passionate embrace. For an instant, she forgot about the vow she had taken before her marriage and envied the couple their love and the luxuries they obviously possessed.

By the time she reached home, her husband had already realized through his spiritual powers that she had broken her vow. Losing his temper along with his common sense, he roared, 'I warned you, Renuka! You know the punishment for this. Why, oh why, did you marry me?'

In fury, Jamadagni ordered his children, one by one, to kill their mother, but they all refused.

Parashurama, who had just arrived home, immediately sensed the tension in the air and asked his father, 'What's the matter?'

The sage replied, 'Will you help me, son?'

'Of course! I promise I will do whatever it is you need me to do.'

'You must kill your mother,' said the sage.

Reluctantly, Parashurama nodded and executed his father's orders.

After the deed was done, Jamadagni said, 'I can only imagine how hard that was for you, my son. Ask me whatever you desire and I will give it to you.'

'Bring my mother back and erase the memory of this tragedy from her mind. That is all I ask,' replied Parashurama instantly.

Sage Jamadagni smiled and brought Renuka back to life.

Years later, when Jamadagni was performing penance, Kartavirya Arjuna, the ruler of the land, came to visit him in the ashram. Arjuna was known for his cruel nature.

Despite the king's reputation, the sage took care of him and his retinue in the grand fashion that the king was accustomed to.

Arjuna was surprised to see such prosperity in a sage's home. 'Tell me, how can you afford to treat my men so grandly?'

'The truth is, I have been blessed with a wonderful cow, Nandini, the daughter of the divine Kamadhenu. She gives us whatever we need, but we don't use her for our needs every day. As a hermit, my disciples and family lead a simple life. We don't have property, we don't store anything or buy anything that is not absolutely essential. However, when guests like you come to my home, I request Nandini to fulfil their desires. If there is anything you admire in my humble home, it is not mine but rather Nandini's gift to you.'

'That is simply wonderful, dear Jamadagni,' said the king, while in his heart, he was consumed by envy. 'I must own this cow,' he thought. 'She will be helpful to our army in times of war.'

Arjuna turned to the sage and asked, 'Will you give Nandini to me? In return, I will always give you whatever you want.'

Jamadagni shook his head. 'Nandini is not to be used for material gains, my king. She is meant to live in a sage's abode.'

The king returned to his palace unhappy. Once he was home, he told his family about the magical cow. His commander and children decided that they must possess the cow, no matter the cost.

The king's soldiers stormed the ashram and took the cow by force. When Jamadagni tried to stop them, the soldiers killed him.

Parashurama, who had been away from the ashram that day, came back to find his mother beside herself and his brothers in deep sorrow. When he learnt what had happened, he vowed to avenge his father with his powerful axe, by defeating Kartavirya Arjuna as well as all the arrogant and ruthless kings he could lay his hands on.

From that day onwards, he was called Parashurama, from the word *parasu*, which means axe. He conquered the world sixteen times and gave away the land and treasures to ascetics.

Himself an avatar of Vishnu, Parashurama meets another avatar—Rama—during Sita's *swayamvara*. The challenge of the swayamvara was to lift and string the bow Shivadhanush. When Rama broke the bow in half, Parashurama realized that his time as an avatar had ended and he went to meditate in the mountains of Mahendra.

The White Horseman

Kalki is supposed to be the last avatar of Lord Vishnu. When the evil in the world outweighs the good, Vishnu will come charging on a white horse with a blazing sword. He will remove the darkness of the era and begin a new one. This avatar is yet to come.

Three Mortal Lifetimes

Vishnu's abode in Vaikuntha was guarded by two demigods named Jaya and Vijaya. The guards were devoted to their lord and proud of their job because they could see the lord every day and almost any time they wanted.

Now, Brahma had created a group of special beings called the Sanath Kumars. The Kumars were very learned and pure of heart, and even though they were extremely powerful and mature, they were somehow small in size and looked like young children.

One day, four Kumars came knocking on Vishnu's door.

Jaya and Vijaya immediately accosted them at the entrance, thinking that they were just pesky children. 'You can't come in at this time,' they said. 'The lord is resting.'

The Kumars were surprised by this behaviour, but they said patiently, 'We are great followers of the lord. We love him and we know that he doesn't mind his devotees visiting him at any time. Please inform him that we are here.'

'I'm sorry, but we haven't received any instructions to let you through,' said Jaya and Vijaya firmly.

The discussion soon escalated into a heated argument.

Finally, Jaya and Vijaya barked in frustration, 'You are only children! Who are you to tell us what to do?'

This was the last straw. The Kumars' patience ran out and they cursed the two guards. 'You have let your roles as Vishnu's guards go to your heads. It is your arrogance that makes you treat us this way. May you be born on earth as mortals and live far away from Vishnu.'

Suddenly, the door opened and Vishnu came out, having heard the commotion. He recognized the Kumars the moment he saw them and also understood what had passed.

'Why did you stop them from entering my abode?' he questioned his guards. 'It is a great honour that these special sages have come to visit me.'

Jaya and Vijaya realized their mistake—they fell at the Kumars' feet. 'Please forgive us,' they begged. 'Save us from your curse.'

'Once a curse has been uttered, it cannot be taken back,' said the Kumars. Then they paused and continued, 'But we can give you two choices—you can either be born as friends of the lord and complete seven lives on earth, or you can be born as his enemies for three lifetimes and die at his hands.'

Jaya and Vijaya looked at each other and immediately knew what their decision would be: 'We can't stay away from the lord for seven lifetimes. If we are born as his sworn enemies, then we will recall him every moment of every day. We choose to be born as his enemies for three lifetimes,' they said and bowed.

Vishnu smiled. 'Arrogance has its penalty. I hope you have understood that. Your punishment begins now.'

Hiranyaksha and Hiranyakashipu

Jaya and Vijaya were born as Hiranyaksha and Hiranyakashipu, the sons of the sage Kashyapa. The two brothers were powerful asuras and the rulers of their land. They were known for their bravado and cruelty. They loathed Vishnu with an unbridled passion and were possessed by a fierce desire to destroy him. As a result, they would often torment Vishnu's devotees.

Unable to take it any more, the people of the land flocked to Vishnu. 'O lord! You teach us to be kind and pious and helpful to others, but the asuras don't follow your ways at all. They torment us every chance they get and we live in constant fear of them. We need your help.'

Vishnu smiled and said, 'Do not worry. I will take care of this.'

True to his word, the next time the yellow-eyed asura Hiranyaksha ordered his soldiers to plunder the homes in his kingdom, Vishnu took the form of a wild boar—Varaha—and came down to earth, stopping the soldiers from entering the homes.

When Hiranyaksha heard the news, he was shocked. 'That's ridiculous! How can a wild boar be a match for my soldiers?'

He sent a stronger army to defeat Varaha. While the boar was decimating Hiranyaksha's army, the asura kidnapped Bhu Devi, in an attempt to take over the world, and imprisoned her in the ocean.

Hearing Bhu Devi's cries, Vishnu—still in the form of Varaha—rushed to rescue her. The duel between the well-armed Hiranyaksha and the weaponless wild boar lasted many years. It was a fierce match, but finally, the boar killed Hiranyaksha, saving Bhu Devi and consequently the earth from his dark rule.

Thus Vishnu fulfilled his prophecy in the avatar of Varaha.

People everywhere sighed with relief and contentment, happy to have got rid of Hiranyaksha. However, there was still Hiranyakashipu to be dealt with.

At the time of Hiranyaksha's death, Hiranyakashipu had been away from the kingdom. When he came back and learnt about his brother's fate, Hiranyakashipu immediately departed for the realm of the gods and performed a severe penance to please Brahma.

Delighted with his sincerity, Brahma revealed himself and asked Hiranyakashipu, 'What do you desire, my beloved devotee?'

Like almost every other asura, Hiranyakashipu replied, 'I want to be immortal.'

Brahma refused, as usual.

'In that case,' said Hiranyakashipu, 'please bless me so that I cannot die at the hands of a human or an animal, in the morning or at night, inside or outside the house.'

'So be it,' said Brahma.

Hiranyakashipu's wife, Kayadhu, who was pregnant with their child at the time, was a kind and devout woman. She did not approve of her husband's ways and was forever begging him not to trouble his subjects.

One day, while Hiranyakashipu was away from the capital in his quest to conquer other kingdoms, Indra invaded the city.

Kayadhu had no choice but to flee. On the way, she met the travelling sage Narada, who took pity on her and offered her a place to stay—his ashram—until things settled down. Kayadhu was grateful for the shelter.

As Narada was an ardent follower of Vishnu, the ashram was filled with prayers and bhajans sung in Vishnu's praise. The child in Kayadhu's womb could hear all this as well as all the stories of Vishnu's glory. By the time the child was born, he was already devoted to Vishnu. Sage Narada fondly named the newborn Prahlada.

Meanwhile, Hiranyakashipu had seized many kingdoms and come back victorious to his capital, only to find out that Indra had destroyed his palace and that his wife now resided in Narada's ashram. He rushed to the ashram to see his wife and son and, after thanking the sage profusely, brought his family back to the capital.

Hiranyakashipu was furious at the gods, and his vendetta against Vishnu in particular grew more intense. He thought, 'Indra had the gall to ruin my home and capital in my absence only because of Vishnu's support. Vishnu is my enemy and from this day on, I will not allow anyone to say his name in my kingdom.'

Years passed and Prahlada grew into a happy and cheerful child. Still a Vishnu devotee, he would keep chanting, 'Vishnu is the best supreme being.'

When he went to his *gurukul*, his teacher tried his best to dissuade him from chanting that, following Hiranyakashipu's instructions, but Prahlada smiled and said simply, 'That is not the truth.' No matter what anyone said, he just repeated what he had learnt when he was in his mother's womb back at Narada's ashram.

Once, when he was visiting his parents, his father took the boy in his arms and asked him affectionately, 'My child, you must have studied many things in your gurukul. Tell me, what have you learnt?'

'Dear father, Vishnu is the greatest force that exists. He is kind and forgiving, and we should be the same. If you have faith in him, the journey of life will become much easier.'

Shaken by what he had just heard, Hiranyakashipu threw Prahlada to the ground. Kayadhu came running to find out what was happening and was alarmed to see her husband's face red with anger.

Prahlada, however, was not perturbed. He just picked himself up, folded his hands and began chanting, 'Om Narayana.'

Hiranyakashipu summoned his son's gurus and questioned them, 'What have you been teaching my young son? One of you is responsible for putting these thoughts into his head! How dare you teach my child to chant the name of my sworn enemy? Tell me, who is the culprit? He will be punished severely!'

'No, sir,' replied the scared teachers. 'We haven't taught him anything about Vishnu. In fact, he is the one who teaches *us*. The truth is that he is a good boy and we have never seen him throw a tantrum or take advantage of his princely status. He studies all subjects equally diligently and we have no complaints except one—he refuses to listen to us when it comes to Vishnu. Otherwise, he is the picture of perfection.'

Hiranyakashipu calmed down and thought for a while. Finally he decided to give Prahlada's teachers another chance to take the boy's mind off Vishnu.

Time passed but nothing changed, and Hiranyakashipu soon lost his patience. 'How can my own flesh and blood chant my enemy's name day and night? If my subjects come to learn of this, they will lose their respect for me. I must teach Prahlada a lesson.'

Later, when Prahlada came to see his father, Hiranyakashipu said to him, 'I must punish you severely for your blind faith in Vishnu. I cannot spare you simply because you are my son. You are completely mistaken, Prahlada. He is not the supreme being nor will he ever come to your rescue.'

Prahlada only said calmly, 'Do what you will with me, Father, but I know that Vishnu will save me.'

'My soldiers will accompany you to the closest mountain range and push you down from the highest peak.'

Hiranyakashipu was sure that Prahlada would be frightened at the mere thought of being pushed from a high mountain and thus recant his beliefs.

Kayadhu was aghast at what was happening. She cried and pleaded with her husband. 'Don't be cruel. He's just a child . . . *your* child!'

Hiranyakashipu had never cared for his wife's opinion. Still, he consoled her, saying, 'I love my son as much as you do, but once he sees the view from the top of that mountain, he will understand that I am the one in control. He must realize that his opinions have to be a reflection of mine. Vishnu is responsible for the death of my dearest brother. Our child must understand that he was born an asura, which means that Vishnu will always be our enemy.'

Meanwhile on the mountaintop, Prahlada remained composed and kept chanting Vishnu's name. With no other choice but to follow the king's orders, the soldiers pushed Prahlada from the peak to certain death. But when they reached the bottom of the mountain, the soldiers found Prahlada sitting there safely, still chanting, 'Hari om.'

When Hiranyakashipu heard this, he was filled with rage while Kayadhu was happy that her child had survived. But almost immediately, the relief drained out of her. 'What punishment will the king inflict on my little boy now?' she wondered fearfully.

'It was just Prahlada's luck that saved him. I must think of a more severe punishment,' thought Hiranyakashipu. He then declared, 'Prahlada should be given poison to drink in front of me. Then let's see how his lord saves him.'

The helpless Kayadhu cried inconsolably.

When the time came for Prahlada to drink the poison, he turned to his mother and said, 'Don't worry about me, Mother. There is no reason to. The lord always helps his devotees. For all you know, the poison may turn into nectar!'

He drank the poison cheerfully.

To everyone's astonishment, it was as if he had simply had a drink of water. Nothing happened, and Prahlada survived once again.

His father, however, was not ready to give up. He devised yet another cruel punishment. 'Throw him into a raging fire. I would rather lose a child than have an enemy like him live in the same home as me.'

But Prahlada survived even the flames without so much as a blister.

Hiranyakashipu did not know what to do next. He was frustrated, angry and unable to accept the fact that his child was a true devotee of his enemy.

One day, he called Prahlada to the palace late in the evening and asked him, 'Tell me, son, where is the lord you worship so much? Call out to him. I want to see him.'

'My dear father,' said Prahlada with a smile, 'he is everywhere. There's no place that can be without him.'

'Is that so?' mocked Hiranyakashipu.

'Yes, Father, it is.'

'Is he in this door then? Or what about this window, this wall or that chair?' his father taunted.

'Yes, Father, he's in all the places you mentioned.'

'If that is true, then he must be in this pillar too. Tell him to come out and show me his face,' thundered Hiranyakashipu.

Suddenly, there was a deafening blast and the pillar burst wide open. A creature with the face of a lion and the body of a human emerged from it. It was the god Narasimha, another one of Vishnu's avatars.

Hiranyakashipu tried to fight the creature but he was no match for the god, of course. Narasimha grabbed the king and held him down in the doorway, so Hiranyakashipu was neither inside the house nor outside. At that time, it was neither morning nor evening—it was twilight. Narasimha had thus fulfilled all the conditions of Brahma's boon and within minutes, he killed Hiranyakashipu.

An intense silence fell upon the palace.

Narasimha approached Prahlada and said with love, 'You will be remembered as one of my greatest devotees on earth. When people think of me, they will think of you too. Against all odds, you stuck to your faith in me. You are the supreme soul. May you have all the kingdoms you deserve and rule them wisely. You will be prosperous and much loved . . . and I will always be with you.'

Thus the first mortal births of Jaya and Vijaya in the form of enemies of the lord came to an end.

Ravana and Kumbhakarna

All of us are aware of the story of the great epic Ramayana, in which Ravana of Lanka kidnaps Sita, Rama's wife. This led to the great war between Rama and Ravana. King Ravana had a brother named Kumbhakarna. He was a giant—mighty and powerful—who slept continuously for six months in a year. When the war began, Ravana forced him to wake up from his slumber and asked him for his help to slay Rama. Kumbhakarna advised him against it. King Ravana, however, refused to listen to him and insisted that Kumbhakarna fulfil his brotherly duty. So the giant went off to the battlefield, only to be killed by Rama, an avatar of Vishnu. In the end, Ravana himself fought a fierce battle with Rama but died, as was his destiny.

This is how the second mortal lives of Jaya and Vijaya, as Ravana and Kumbhakarna, finally ended.

Shishupala and Dantavakra

Damaghosh, king of Chedi, and his wife, Srutadevi, were extremely sad when their child was born.

The newborn prince, who was named Shishupala, was very ugly—he had four hands and three eyes. Everybody stared at him with veiled disgust. His parents worried about his future; they wondered if Shishupala would be able to rule the kingdom once he reached adulthood.

After some thought, the king invited learned people from all over the kingdom for advice on what could be done.

Some people suggested, 'Abandon him in the forest. He is a bad omen for the kingdom.'

'Put him in a boat and let the boat sail away,' said the others.

'Why don't you just give him away to someone who will raise him quietly?'

But neither the king nor the queen accepted these as solutions. He was their son and they loved him, irrespective of his appearance.

One day, an old man came to see the child. He advised Srutadevi, 'O my queen, be strong. Your child will become normal and lose the extra hands and eye when he sits in the lap of a special person, who is yet to visit your palace.'

Srutadevi was ecstatic.

Then the old man averted his eyes. 'But . . .'

'What is it?' asked Srutadevi, concerned.

'This same person will also be responsible for the death of your son.'

The queen's eyes filled with tears. 'What can we do? Is there any way to stop it?' she asked.

'I don't know,' said the old man gently. 'You should ask the man himself when he comes here.'

For the next few months, Srutadevi placed her child in the lap of all who visited the palace, but nothing happened and the extra hands and eye remained.

One day, Srutadevi's nephew, Krishna, came to visit his aunt. Srutadevi promptly placed the baby in his lap. Immediately, all the extra appendages disappeared and the child became normal. The moment was bittersweet for the queen, who now worried about her son's death. She said, 'My dear Krishna, you have given my son a new lease of life. But I also know that you will be the cause of his death. Please, I beg you, spare my son.'

Krishna was moved by his aunt's grief. 'My dear aunt,' he said, 'I can't see you cry. If I am the one destined to kill your son, then it must be a consequence of some terrible wrongdoing. I don't know the future, but I advise you to ensure that your son follows the right path.'

'I will try my best to raise my son to be a good man, but promise me that you will pardon him for any mistake that he might make.'

'That will not do, beloved aunt. When someone makes a mistake the first time, you can pardon them, and the second time may only require a warning. However, if they repeat their mistake a third time, they must be punished. I can't accept his faults endlessly. There has to be a limit.'

'If that is so, please allow my son a hundred mistakes,' begged Srutadevi.

Krishna nodded and smiled.

Shishupala grew up to be an arrogant prince who had no respect for anyone. He became friends with an evil king called Jarasandha and his cousin Dantavakra, who only led him further astray. When he reached adulthood, he wanted to marry Princess Rukmini though she did not return his feelings. Their marriage, however, was fixed anyway because of his insistence. But on the day of their wedding, she ran away and married Krishna. That was the day Shishupala began to hate his cousin with a vengeance.

Time passed by until one day, Yudhishthira, the oldest of the Pandavas, decided to perform the Rajasuya yagna and honour Krishna. It was a big occasion for all the emperors of India, and Shishupala was one of the attendees. The moment he saw Krishna there and the ceremonies conducted in his honour, Shishupala couldn't restrain the hate in his heart any more and began to hurl abuses at Krishna. Shocked by Shishupala's filthy language, everybody around got up to stop him, but Krishna only smiled and said, 'Please don't worry. Stay calm and sit down.'

Recalling the promise to his aunt, Krishna began counting Shishupala's mistakes. Once the number crossed a hundred, Krishna used his Sudarshan Chakra to kill him.

Shishupala was none other than Jaya and Krishna, yet another avatar of Vishnu. And Vijaya, who was in the form of Dantavakra, was also killed by Vishnu in a duel known as a *gada-yuddha*, in which the only weapon used was the mace.

Thus Jaya and Vijaya completed their three mortal lifetimes and returned to Vaikuntha as Vishnu's gatekeepers.

A Friend in Need

Ashes to Ashes

Once, an asura who was a great devotee of Brahma performed an austere penance to please the god. When Brahma appeared, the asura bowed and said, 'Lord, grant me the power to turn a person into ashes the moment I touch his head with my palm.'

'Why?' asked Brahma.

'With such a boon, I can conquer the world without an army,' replied the asura.

Brahma smiled and blessed him. 'So be it. From this day on, you will be known as Bhasmasura.'

The moment Bhasmasura acquired the power he had asked for he decided that he wanted to defeat the Trinity so no one could stand in his way.

A wicked plan hatched in his mind, and he resolved to implement it soon. He wanted to keep his palm on Brahma's head and destroy him. Even as the plan took shape in Bhasmasura's mind, Brahma realized the asura's malicious intent through his divine powers. Lord Brahma was shocked! He had never imagined that his boon would be used against him. Brahma had no choice but to flee as fast and as far as he could—with Bhasmasura right behind him.

The chase lasted for months. While on the run, Brahma finally called out to Vishnu, 'Help me! You must protect me or the balance of the whole world will be in danger!'

'If that's the case, you should think twice before granting such boons,' replied Vishnu.

'But I am bound by the affection of my devotees and compelled to give them what they desire. After all, I am their father and creator. But I also know that you are always there to help me,' said Brahma.

'Hmm,' said Vishnu non-committally.

Bhasmasura, who had been in hot pursuit of Brahma and was about to exit the earthly realm, came to a sudden halt. He had just spotted an exquisite woman strolling in a garden nearby. Forgetting all about Brahma, Bhasmasura inched towards the maiden. The closer he got, the more enchanted he became. He hadn't seen such a beauty in his life! Even the apsaras Menaka and Rambha couldn't hold a candle to her.

The maiden smiled politely when she found the asura standing right in front of her.

'O enchanting lady, you must be the most beautiful woman in the world,' he said. 'I am Bhasmasura and I have the power to reduce anyone to a heap of ashes. Everyone, including Brahma, is afraid of me. I wish to marry you.'

The maiden's smile widened.

Bhasmasura continued, 'You are fortunate to have found someone like me. If you agree to be my queen, you will find the whole world waiting on you. I can make any deva or king listen to you and fulfil all your desires. But first, tell me, what is your name?'

The maiden bowed. 'My lord, my name is Mohini. I am indeed fortunate to have a suitor like you. But there is something you must know about me. I . . . happen to be an extraordinary dancer and—'

'What is it, my dear Mohini? What is the problem?' Bhasmasura interrupted impatiently.

'I have taken a vow that whomever I marry must also be a good dancer. I don't have any other condition. I will not dare to demand anything else from you.'

Bhasmasura felt awkward and a little helpless. 'I don't know how to dance, Mohini,' he admitted. 'But I can make other people dance to your tunes.'

'O Bhasmasura, it is nothing! A person like you can learn to dance quickly and easily. If you like, I can be your guru. Will you at least allow me to teach you for a few minutes? I am confident you will be an expert in no time. It will make me very happy if you agree to do this for me.'

Bhasmasura looked at Mohini. Her bright brown eyes twinkled at him, and Bhasmasura was immediately convinced that she was telling the truth about her vow. He thought, 'If I dance a little with her, she will most likely agree to marry me. With her beauty and my might, we will make the most perfect couple in the world and rule over everyone!'

He nodded.

Without further ado, Mohini began the lesson. 'Turn your foot to the left and take a step forward like this,' she said.

Bhasmasura tried to mirror her moves.

'Now come this way and take two steps to the right.'

After a few minutes, she exclaimed with happiness, 'You are such an excellent student. I'm afraid you will become an even better dancer than me!'

Bhasmasura was overjoyed and continued to follow her movements.

Then Mohini suggested, 'Let me teach you a few hand movements and postures now.'

'Of course,' agreed Bhasmasura.

'Stretch out your left hand and hold it this way,' she said, showing him the stance.

Her instructions now became more demanding and came quickly, one after the other.

'Extend your right hand.

'Rotate the left wrist.

'Now do the same with the other hand.

'Now spread your left hand outwards and extend your right leg until it looks like this.' She demonstrated promptly as she moved on to the next instruction. 'Now do the same action with the opposite hand and leg.'

Bhasmasura tried to copy her as best as he could, but he was a terrible dancer. There was nothing graceful about him.

And yet, Mohini looked at him in awe. 'Oh my God! You are dancing like a bird. You are agile and your swiftness is unmatched. Now let's try something a little more complicated.'

Bhasmasura beamed.

'Take your right hand and put it on your waist. Put your left hand on your waist as well,' Mohini said.

Bhasmasura followed her instructions meekly.

'Now put your right hand on your shoulder, and then your left hand too. Look at me and repeat,' she said, smiling at her student.

'Swing your left hand back and forth, and place the right hand on your head. And go around in a circle like this,' said Mohini, demonstrating.

Bhasmasura was so busy looking at her and appreciating her expertise that he swung his left hand and placed the right one on his head blindly, without realizing what was going to happen. Within seconds, he was reduced to a heap of ashes.

And Mohini instantly transformed into Vishnu!

Many paintings and statues depict this incident, which is popularly known as Mohini Bhasmasura. The most captivating of them can be viewed in the temple of Belur in Karnataka, where Mohini is portrayed as dancing with her right hand on her head.

The Elephant and the Crocodile

There once lived a king named Indradyumna, who was a devotee of Vishnu.

One day, the great sage Agastya came to visit Indradyumna on a hot summer's day. At the palace, the king did not bother to attend to Agastya or offer him something to drink. The sage was tired, thirsty and hungry, and so he was reasonably upset by the king's disrespectful behaviour.

The enraged Agastya cursed the king. 'May you be born as an elephant in your next life and search desperately for water to quench your thirst.'

The king realized his folly and begged for forgiveness. 'I am really sorry for my behaviour. Please take back the curse!'

The sage said, 'I cannot do that, but I grant that you will return to your true form when the lord comes for you.'

In another part of the world, a handsome gandharva was bathing in a river with his wife, when the sage Devala passed by. The gandharva threw some water at him playfully and asked him to join them. Devala, however, was livid at the gandharva's immaturity and cursed him. 'May you be born as a crocodile in your next birth,' shouted the sage.

Thus, the poor gandharva was reborn as a crocodile.

Meanwhile, Agastya's curse also came to pass and Indradyumna was reborn as an elephant. He eventually became the king of elephants and was called Gajendra.

One day, Gajendra was in his favourite lake with his herd, when suddenly something caught hold of one of his feet under the water. It turned out to be a monstrous crocodile! Gajendra was aware of his own strength and was sure that no animal could continue to hold him for long. But to his surprise, no amount of struggle could loosen his foot from the jaws of the crocodile. He called out to his relatives and friends for help, but even they couldn't get him free. After hours and days, they all left, leaving Gajendra alone in the lake with the crocodile.

All of a sudden, he had a vision of his past life as Indradyumna and the memories came flooding back.

Gajendra started praying to Vishnu. 'There is no one in the universe but you whom I can call upon. Please help me, O lord! I used to think that I was very powerful and strong, but now I realize that nothing is in my hands. I know that you help your devotees when they are in distress, so I will pray and wait for you, no matter how long it takes.'

Finally, Vishnu appeared and launched his Sudarshan Chakra at the crocodile. The creature was killed and, in its place, the gandharva who had been cursed appeared, back in his true form. Gajendra also transformed back to Indradyumna.

This incident is frequently referred to as Gajendra Moksha and is said to have occurred on top of the Tirumala Hills in Tirupati.

The Man from the Egg

The sage Kashyapa is considered to be one of the seven holy rishis and the father of all living species. One day, Sage Kashyapa said to his wives Kadru and Vinata, 'I would like to give you each a boon. Tell me, what do you want the most?'

Kadru smiled and said, 'Bless me with a thousand sons.'

The sage nodded and then turned to Vinata.

'Dear husband, I want two sons who will be stronger than all the sons of Kadru,' said Vinata.

'So be it,' said Kashyapa, blessing both the women.

In time, Kadru and Vinata both laid eggs. Kadru's children hatched first, and that is how the first nagas, or the serpent tribe, came to be. The oldest of them was Adisesha, who forms the bed that Vishnu lies on, and he was followed by Vasuki, who would later become the king of snakes.

Vinata waited and waited, but her eggs showed no sign of hatching.

One day, when the two women were out for a stroll on the seashore, Vinata spotted Uchaishravas, the seven-headed horse that had emerged from the churning of the ocean, flying in the sky.

Vinata exclaimed, 'Kadru, look at that horse! It is absolutely snow-white. How beautiful it is!'

Kadru looked at the horse galloping away from them in the darkening skies. 'No, Vinata,' she said. 'Can't you see? His tail is black.'

By the time they both glanced at the sky again, Uchaishravas had vanished.

Vinata was certain that the horse was unquestionably white and said so to Kadru. Kadru was now not so sure about the tail being black, but she was too proud to admit that she may have been wrong. The two argued for some time, and in the end, they decided to bet on it and agreed to return to the seashore at the same time the next day, in the hope that Uchaishravas would return.

The bet was simple. If the horse's tail was black, Vinata would become Kadru's slave and if it wasn't, Kadru would become Vinata's slave.

Late that night, Kadru called her children and told them about the wager. Some of her children remarked, 'Mother, you are wrong. Uchaishravas does not have a black tail. It is all-white. You are going to lose.'

Kadru was worried—she did not want to become Vinata's slave. 'Will you not help your mother?' she asked her children. 'Some of you can cover Uchaishravas's tail, and because you are serpents, you will appear black from a distance. You only have to stay there for as long as Vinata and I look at the horse. After that, you can return. I can't afford to lose this bet!'

'You can't cheat someone like that, Mother. After all, you are the one who always tells us to be fair and truthful,' they protested.

But the idea of being Vinata's slave was too humiliating. Kadru cried out in anger, 'I will become a slave because of all of you! Well, since you don't want to protect your own mother, I curse you with death. All of you will be destroyed in a mighty Sarpa yagna.'[10]

Only one serpent, Karkotaka, agreed to help his mother.

The next day, Vinata and Kadru went to the seashore to see Uchaishravas; and there he was, happily flying around in the sky. This time, both of them could see that the horse had a black tail.

Not suspecting any foul play, Vinata admitted that she had lost and became Kadru's slave.

Kadru said, 'Your slavery will come to an end only when your future son brings nectar from the heavens and revives my children, who will all perish one day. Until then, you must remain my slave.'

Vinata had no choice but to agree.

Years passed by, and Vinata's eggs still didn't hatch. Tired of being a slave to Kadru and overcome by frustration, Vinata decided that she couldn't wait any longer and used her hands to gently break one of eggs. To her surprise and distress, she found a beautiful boy inside the egg with undeveloped legs.

'Mother,' he said sadly, 'I am glad to see you, but why were you in such a hurry to break this egg? Good things take

---

[10] Her prophecy would come true much later, during the reign of Janmejaya in the kingdom of Hastinapur, when the serpents would be sacrificed as revenge for his father's death. Janmejaya was the successor of Parikshit, grandson of the Pandava Arjuna.

time and your impatience has cost me my legs. Now I will not be able to retrieve the nectar to free you.'

Vinata cried out, 'My dear child, you have suffered because of my mistake! Please forgive me. Where will you go? Who will look after you? I wish you would stay here with me.'

'No, Mother, I must leave. I will become the charioteer of the sun god. I will manage his seven horses and ride from dawn to dusk. It is the best job for me, as I won't really need to walk.'

'When will I see you, my child?' pleaded Vinata, still upset over losing her son so soon.

'Every morning, Mother. I will be known as Aruna, and I will accompany the sun god every day. I implore you not to be impatient next time. If you can wait a little longer, you will be blessed with another son, who will bring you your freedom.'

Aruna then left his mother to fulfil his destiny as Surya's charioteer. This is why the sunrise is also known as *arunodaya*, or 'the coming of Aruna'.

After this incident, Vinata took care of the second egg as best as she could and the guilt from her past mistake restrained her from forcing it to hatch. Months and years passed.

Finally, one day, the egg broke and a strong-winged, healthy bird-faced man emerged from it. 'Mother, I have arrived,' he declared. 'Thanks to your patience, I am strong and can fly anywhere. I am the mighty Garuda. I will be the primary vehicle of Lord Vishnu and his consort, Lakshmi. I promise to free you from your slavery.'

Without another word, he soared high up in the sky, while his mother watched him from below with pride, happy to finally see him and reassured by his promise.

She had waited long for her freedom.

Without another word, he soared high up in the sky, while his mother watched him from below with pride, happy to finally see him and reassured by his promise.

She had waited long for her freedom.

The Forked Tongues

Garuda was born with great might and intellect. Also known as Vainateya, the son of Vinata, Garuda knew that the only way to free his mother from slavery was to bring the nectar of immortality to Kadru. As the pot of nectar was in the possession of Indra, Garuda requested the king of the gods to give it to him.

Indra, however, refused. He knew that the price the world had paid for nectar was high and he could not just hand it over to Garuda.

Garuda had no choice but to fight Indra.

Indra used the weapon Vajrayudha to try and cut off Garuda's wings, but the weapon only managed to snip off one of his feathers. Garuda remained unharmed and as strong as ever. Indra was simply no match for Garuda, so he ran to Vishnu with the nectar. Vishnu assured him that he would take care of the pot and sent Indra back home.

Just as Indra left, Garuda came to Vishnu asking for the pot of nectar. When Vishnu did not agree, Garuda attacked him. Vishnu understood that the nectar meant freedom for Garuda's mother but, for the sake of mankind, there was no way he could part with it. If the pot went to Kadru, she could give it to whomever she wanted and the long-term consequences had great potential to diminish the survival of the human race. So Vishnu fought back fiercely.

By the end of the day, Garuda and Vishnu were both tired and there was no winner in sight.

Vishnu appreciated Garuda's spirit and devotion to his mother. He said, 'Young one, though you are my opponent in this fight, it brings me joy to witness your power. I wish to give you a boon. Ask me for whatever you desire, except the nectar.'

Happy to hear Vishnu's words, Garuda bowed and said, 'I am blessed indeed to have the opportunity to fight you as an equal. Though I am not a great person, allow me to give you a boon as well. Please tell me what you want.'

Vishnu smiled, 'As I am older than you, I will ask for my boon first. I want you to be my devotee and my eternal vehicle. In your honour, I will also be known as Garuda Vahana.' This way, Vishnu could always keep an eye on Garuda.

Garuda smiled and agreed. 'O lord, to be allowed to carry you throughout my life is truly my privilege,' he said. 'However, now it is my turn. I wish to always be above you.'

'Of course! The flag above me that heralds my arrival will now forever have your image imprinted on it, and hence, your condition will be met. The flag will be called Garuda Dhwaja.'

Thus, the battle ended on a happy note.

Now that an agreement had been reached, Vishnu calmly explained the consequences of handing over the nectar to Garuda.

'Lord,' said Garuda, 'I only want to rescue my mother from Kadru's clutches. I beg you, please do something!'

'Very well. Take this pot of nectar, hand it over to Kadru and set your mother free. However, you will not question my actions after that,' Vishnu replied firmly.

So Garuda offered the pot to Kadru, who said, 'You have done your duty. I am pleased. Vinata is now free from slavery.'

After rescuing his mother, Garuda took to the sky for his next task for Vishnu.

Meanwhile, Vishnu had already set his plan to recover the nectar in motion.

Indra went to Kadru in disguise. Knowing just how precious the nectar was, Kadru was clutching the pot rather tightly.

'It must be wonderful to possess the gift of immortality,' said Indra. 'However, before you distribute this among your children, is it not one's duty to cleanse themselves before they drink something so pure?'

Kadru was so euphoric that she was easily convinced. 'Let us first go have a bath,' she said to her children, and they all went to the nearest river.

Indra seized the opportunity to grab the pot of nectar and ran back to his abode. Unfortunately, he spilt a few drops of the liquid on a pile of hay that was lying outside Kadru's home.

A few of the snakes managed to finish their bath early and came looking for the nectar, but alas, the pot was no

longer there! But when they noticed a few drops on the hay, they quickly licked off what they could before their brothers arrived. The hay was dry and its edges were sharp, so as the snakes licked the nectar, the edges cut their tongues, almost splitting them into two.

These are the only snakes that exist in the world today, and now you know why they have forked tongues!

The Honest Cheater

One day, Indra went to visit Shiva on Mount Kailash. But instead of Shiva, he found an unfamiliar person there, deep in meditation. 'That must be one of Shiva's *ganas*,' he thought. He said aloud, 'I want to meet your master. Where is he?'

The man did not reply.

Indra tried again and again, but there was no response. 'I am the king of the gods,' thought Indra, feeling insulted. 'How dare he ignore me?' He picked up the Vajrayudha and threw it at the man.

Finally, the man opened his eyes and, annoyed by the disturbance, shot a fiery arrow at Indra, while transforming into Shiva. That's when Indra realized that Shiva had simply been meditating in an altered form. Scared for his life, Indra begged him for forgiveness.

Shiva calmed down just in time to redirect the arrow towards the ocean. The arrow fell into the deep waters and manifested itself as a crying baby boy. The king of the ocean heard the wailing and decided to adopt the newborn. He asked Brahma to suggest a name for the child.

'Call him Jalandhara, the boy born out of water,' replied Brahma. 'He will not be destroyed by anyone other than Shiva as it was his arrow responsible for the boy's creation—that's my boon to him.'

Jalandhara grew up into a fine young man, and the king of the ocean crowned him the ruler of the asuras. Jalandhara was a fair and just king, and he married a beautiful girl named Brinda.

One day, a few old asuras visited Jalandhara and told him about the churning of the ocean and how Vishnu had cheated them out of the nectar in the guise of Mohini. Enraged by the deception, Jalandhara swore to take revenge on the gods.

Brinda was a devotee of Vishnu; she advised her husband not to wage war on the gods, but he did not heed her words. So there was nothing else she could do but pray fervently to Vishnu for Jalandhara's safe return.

It was a fierce battle, and just when Indra was about to land a terrible blow on Jalandhara's head, Vishnu's Sudarshan Chakra came to protect him and Indra had no choice but to run away.

Jalandhara now knew that he had two advantages. Not only was he almost unmatched in strength, but he was always protected by Vishnu because of Brinda's prayers. Soon, Jalandhara began conquering kingdom after kingdom in all the realms.

His victories made him so proud that, one day, he decided to fight Vishnu himself.

Vishnu did not want to fight him because of Brinda, so he tried to handle Jalandhara in a tactful manner, 'It's not that I can't fight you. However, the fact is that you are born from the ocean and thus you are like a brother to my wife, Lakshmi, who also emerged from the ocean. I do not wish to fight my wife's brother.'

Jalandhara was speechless. He had never thought of Vishnu as his brother-in-law! He replied, 'May my sister and you be happy forever.'

Now that that was settled, Jalandhara decided to go to war with Shiva. Jalandhara had forgotten who was responsible for his birth or the blessings he had received as an infant.

Brinda tried to stop her husband. 'Please don't do this! You will never win against Shiva.'

But Jalandhara, as usual, refused to listen and left for Mount Kailash.

This time, Brinda knew that there was a chance her husband might not return, and so she again prayed to Vishnu with all her heart and soul.

Jalandhara reached Shiva's abode and roared, 'Mount Kailash now belongs to me! If you surrender, I will allow you to leave and reside elsewhere.'

Shiva thought for a bit. He was reluctant to slay Jalandhara, who was technically his son and under Vishnu's protection. However, Shiva was also aware that Jalandhara had gone over to the dark side.

When the news reached Vishnu, he thought to himself, 'I can't protect Jalandhara forever. Brinda is the epitome of all that is good, and she is the strength behind Jalandhara's triumph and his continued well-being. The gods can only defeat him by deceiving Brinda.'

So Vishnu disguised himself as Jalandhara and went to his palace to meet Brinda. 'My dear wife,' he said, 'I have won the war. You need not pray to Vishnu any more. Instead, prepare for an extravagant celebration.'

Brinda was ecstatic to see her husband and learn of his victory. She stopped praying and began to plan the festivities.

Shiva realized what had taken place—Brinda had stopped her prayers. He seized the opportunity to use his trident and kill Jalandhara.

When Brinda found out about how Vishnu had misled her, she was furious. 'How could you trick your own devotee?' she cried out. 'It is heartless . . . and your heart must be made of stone. Well, may you turn into one then!'

Vishnu smiled at her and said, 'Brinda, there is nothing wrong with deceiving someone for the greater good, and I had no choice, for while you were good and sincere, your husband was not. He hurt many sages, scholars and his own subjects. However, I accept your curse with all my heart, my child. I will turn into a *shaligrama* near River Gandaki. Whenever someone wants to worship my form, they can pick up a shaligrama from the river and pray to me, and I will always hear them. Despite all that has happened, your devotion has pleased me. You will be reborn as a tulsi plant, and my worship will only be complete with tulsi leaves In fact, you will be worshipped before me. People will revere you for your piety and keep tulsi plants in their homes, where you will bring prosperity.'

This is why it is common to see the tulsi plant in many Indian homes.

The Choice of Death

Madhu and Kaitabha were two asura brothers who once prayed to Goddess Parvati in the hope of attaining immortality. But Parvati, like the other gods, denied their request. However, taking pity on them, she said, 'I will give you one more chance to ask for something more reasonable.'

The two brothers looked at each other. 'In that case, we want to die at the time of our choosing,' they said cleverly, absolutely sure that they would never wish to die.

Parvati smiled. 'So be it.'

Like all other power-hungry asuras, the two brothers soon became evil and insufferable. They seized whatever they wanted and killed whoever tried to stop them.

One day, they went to meet Brahma. The god was sitting high atop his lotus and appeared to be busy sculpting his next creation.

The two brothers were irked to see him so high up. 'Come down, old man!' they said to Brahma. 'Only people with strength and mental fortitude such as ourselves should sit so high. If you want to stay up there, fight and defeat us first. Come down now! We are ready whenever you are!'

Brahma knew that he could not fight them and win, and so he simply ran away.

The two brothers were happy to have humiliated the eternal creator.

Brahma, in the meantime, kept running without looking back even once, until he reached Vishnu and related everything that had happened. 'Lord, if these two asuras can behave so badly with me, imagine how they must be treating other beings. You must destroy them!'

As Vishnu pondered over the situation, Madhu and Kaitabha reached Vaikuntha in search of Brahma. When they saw Vishnu, they smirked and said, 'O great Vishnu, how can you protect another when you yourself are so weak compared to us?'

Without waiting for an answer, the asuras looked around Vaikuntha and liked what they saw. 'Why don't you give your abode to us?' they demanded. 'We are more suitable inhabitants. Come, we will allow you to try to defeat us first.'

'Then let us fight,' agreed Vishnu placidly.

As the sparring began, Vishnu reached out to Goddess Parvati with his mind. 'You gave these two asuras such power, so you must be accountable for their actions. I need your help.'

The goddess responded, 'Don't worry, Vishnu. I will enter the asuras' minds and enable you to trick them.'

After the fight had gone on for some time, the two asura warriors wanted to rest. They asked Vishnu, 'Would you like to take a break and rest before we continue?'

'Of course we must rest. We must respect each other as warriors.'

While they were resting, the two brothers looked at Vishnu with pity. 'You have unnecessarily picked a fight with us because of Brahma. We have no enmity with you, so we are very happy to find such a worthy opponent. We would like to bless you with a boon. Tell us what you want.'

They were quite sure that Vishnu's wish from them would be for a truce.

Vishnu instantly realized that this was Parvati's doing. He knew what to do. 'You are both honourable warriors and I am thankful for the boon that you have offered. I desire that both of you perish by my hand,' said Vishnu.

The deed was done and the goddess vanished from the minds of the asuras. Madhu and Kaitabha now realized their folly, but it was too late. A word of honour must be kept and, reluctantly, they agreed to die.

Despite his victory, Vishnu regretted the result of his trickery. So he said to them, 'You may ask me for anything except for your lives, and I will do my best to fulfil it.'

They said, 'O lord! After our death, we wish for a temple each to be built in our names. Since we are devotees of Goddess Parvati, we would like an *eshwaralinga* in each temple too.'

Vishnu nodded, and then executed them with his Sudarshan Chakra.

Later, Madhukeshwara Temple was built on the very spot where the asuras had perished, on the banks of River Varada, and Kaitabeshwara Temple was erected nearby, with a linga in each.

Today, the two temples are in Karnataka and approximately twenty kilometres apart—one is in Banavasi and the other is in Kotepura.

To Marry a Monkey or a Bear

A long time ago, there lived a king named Ambarish, who had a beautiful daughter named Shrimati. She was a charming princess and the king was in search of a good match for her.

Narada, the wandering sage and one of the sons of Brahma, was known to be an eternal bachelor. The thought of marriage had never crossed his mind and he was happy singing the praises of Vishnu while travelling around the world with his tambura.

One day, Narada and a young sage named Parvata went to visit Ambarish. The king asked his family to attend to them with great care.

Princess Shrimati brought some water to the sages. The moment Narada and Parvata saw her, they both fell head over heels in love with the beautiful princess!

Parvata asked Ambarish, 'Your Majesty, are you looking for a suitable husband for the princess?'

'As a matter of fact, yes, respected sage. If you know of a good match for her, please let me know.'

'The truth is, my king, I have fallen in love with your daughter and want to marry her,' said Parvata boldly.

King Ambarish was taken aback. The thought of getting his daughter married to an ascetic had never occurred to him. However, before he could respond, Narada jumped into the conversation, saying, 'O Ambarish, I am also in love with your daughter. I too am ready to marry her.'

Ambarish could not hide his surprise.

Parvata, however, was very upset at Narada's words. 'I am the one who asked for the princess's hand in marriage first and so I must be the one to marry her,' he said. 'Also, I am closer to her in age and thus more suited to be her groom.'

'Yes, but I am your superior both in life and knowledge. The whole world respects me—I am the son of Brahma! It is clear that I am the more deserving candidate,' retorted Narada.

The argument went on until Ambarish decided to intervene. 'Dear sages, I have only one daughter and this is about her future,' he said. 'I suggest that we retire for the day. This will give Shrimati some time to think about your proposals. I invite both of you to come back tomorrow for an official swayamvara, where she will garland the groom of her choice. Until then, I request you both to avoid speaking to her as it would not be fair for either of you to try and sway her.'

King Ambarish's reasonable solution calmed the sages down a little. They agreed to return the next day and honour the princess's decision.

Still, they both left the court unhappy and insecure.

'Maybe Parvata is right,' thought Narada. 'He is younger than me and was the first to propose to her. The princess might just choose him.'

Meanwhile, Parvata wondered, 'Shrimati will most likely pick Narada because of his popularity and lineage. I really think that he has a better chance than I do.'

The thought took root in Parvata's mind and he decided to do something to tilt the scales in his favour. He stole into Vishnu's abode late in the night.

Vishnu was surprised to see him. 'Why are you here in the middle of the night? Has something untoward happened?'

'My lord, I . . . I want to marry Shrimati!' replied Parvata.

'Then go ahead and do that. This discussion must be between Shrimati and you. I have no role to play here.'

Parvata bowed his head. 'My lord,' he said, 'please let me explain. I have come to you in desperate need of a favour. Narada is competing against me for the princess's hand at the swayamvara in the king's court tomorrow. I request you to ensure that when Shrimati looks at Narada, she only sees the face of a monkey.'

Lord Vishnu smiled, amused at the things men did for love, and blessed Parvata, saying, 'As you wish.'

Meanwhile, Narada was lying wide awake in bed, restless and unable to sleep. 'Vishnu will surely help me—I'm his greatest devotee,' he thought.

When Narada knocked on Vishnu's door a few hours later, the god was not surprised and welcomed him with open arms. Yet he asked Narada, 'Why have you come here at this time, my beloved devotee?'

'Lord, Parvata is my rival at the swayamvara for Shrimati's hand tomorrow. Please help me win!'

'O my dear Narada,' said Vishnu. 'The swayamvara is a system that gives the woman the freedom to choose her groom without any pressure from others. If she likes you, I am certain that she will choose you.'

'My lord, the problem is that I want to be sure that she likes me. I beseech you,' pleaded Narada, 'let Parvata's face appear to be that of a bear's whenever Shrimati looks at him.'

Vishnu smiled. 'All right then.'

The next morning, the two sages woke up feeling confident and prepared to face the swayamvara.

King Ambarish's palace was decorated magnificently with flowers, and the one garland that would adorn the groom was displayed prominently.

The two sages sat in their respective seats, each sure of being the chosen one.

At the designated hour, Shrimati and the king approached them. The princess carried the special garland in her hands.

When Shrimati saw the suitors, she whispered to her father, 'Where are the sages? I can only see two beings before me—one with the face of a monkey and the other with the face of a bear!'

King Ambarish wondered what his daughter was talking about. He looked at the sages again. They seemed exactly like they were the day before. He gently replied, 'No, my dear. These are the two sages who want your hand in marriage. Maybe you need to get a closer look at them.'

Shrimati went near the sages but they still had animal faces. So she said to them, 'I don't know who you both are— but you look like a monkey . . . and you look like a bear! My heart won't allow me to pick either one of you. However, I do see one man standing between the two of you.'

Parvata and Narada looked at each other. 'Describe him,' they said in unison.

'I see a handsome man in a yellow dhoti smiling at me. His skin is an ethereal blue and he is holding a conch, a mace, a discus and a lotus—one object in each of his four hands. I am drawn to him for some reason . . . in fact, I wish to marry *him*.'

The sages realized that the man was none other than Vishnu.

'Lord, you have cheated me!' cried out Parvata. 'I asked for Narada's face to look like a monkey's but you changed my face too! Why are you here?'

Narada also said accusingly, 'You betrayed me too! I know why you are here! This was your plan all along. You want to marry the princess yourself!'

As the voices rose, Shrimati quietly put the garland around Vishnu's neck.

The sages said to Vishnu, 'Your deception has hurt us terribly. May you be in the company of bears and monkeys.'

The god nodded. 'When I come to earth as Rama, monkeys and bears will be my greatest friends and supporters. The truth is that I did you both a favour, just as you asked. You have deceived each other. I decided to come here and take part in the swayamvara only after you both approached me with your selfish requests. Now, the bride has chosen me. I don't think you know who Shrimati is, my dear sages. She is an avatar of Lakshmi and can only be with me. Let this incident be a lesson, so you never resort to cheating again.'

Narada and Parvata were truly mortified at their behaviour. They hung their heads in shame and left the palace in silence.

The lesson would not be forgotten.

The Web of Illusion

Sage Narada could travel instantly to any part of the world, whether it was the skies, the earth or below the ground. He did not possess a home or a vehicle, and was notorious for mischievously engineering many misunderstandings. However, he would always side with the truth and his words were taken seriously. His presence was always welcomed by devas, asuras and humans.

Narada advised everyone he met to become a sage like him and constantly pray to Vishnu. This upset his father greatly. Brahma said to his son, 'Look, you are free to do whatever you want to do—you have few responsibilities and almost no attachments, but the common man on earth has much more to worry about and must undergo his share of suffering. Don't think that you know what's best for others, especially when you have no understanding of a mortal life, of marriage and children, of joy and sorrow.'

Narada, however, did not heed his father's words and only smiled mockingly at Brahma before going on his way.

A few days later, Narada visited Vishnu, and his conversation with Brahma came up.

Vishnu smiled mysteriously. Suddenly, he coughed and glanced at his devotee. 'I am very thirsty. Will you please bring me a glass of water from the lake nearby?' the god asked.

Narada promptly went to fetch water, kamandalu in hand. While dipping the water pot into the lake, he saw a series of stunning white steps below the surface of the water. Curiosity got the better of him and he could not resist going down the stairs. As he had the power to wander anywhere, Narada was able to go deep under the water. A short while later, he came across a large palace. A beautiful maiden was sitting in the garden in front, making a garland.

'Who are you?' asked Narada in surprise.

'I am the princess of this palace,' the woman replied.

'Who is this garland for?'

'For Vishnu, of course. I am his devotee and I am getting the garland ready for a puja.'

Narada was charmed by the maiden's devotion and beauty, and he joined her for the puja. By the end of it, he had fallen in love with her and asked her to marry him.

Shyly, she agreed.

The two were married in a grand wedding ceremony and Narada lived in the underwater palace with the princess.

Decades went by, and Narada became the father of sixty children. Life was utterly blissful.

One day, a terrible storm came out of nowhere, and the palace came tumbling down. Narada tried his best to save his family, but failed. One by one, he saw all his children

die before him. Narada and his wife cried bitterly at their helplessness. Suddenly, a big wave emerged and his wife was swept away with it. Before he could react, he found himself staring at the eye of the storm. As Narada held on to a tree for dear life, he remembered Vishnu. 'Please save me, please save me,' he chanted and closed his eyes in preparation for death. He became afraid and realized that the life he had was important to him. He wanted to live.

And then he felt someone tapping on his shoulder. When he opened his eyes, he found Vishnu standing beside him. The storm had subsided and everything was quiet and dry.

'Narada, what is the matter?' asked Vishnu.

'Has the storm passed?' Narada asked him in disbelief.

'Why? What happened?'

Narada sobbed. 'I lost my wife and my children, and now I have nothing! I don't deserve to live without them.'

Vishnu chuckled. 'What are you talking about, dear Narada? I only sent you to fetch some water for me, and here you are sitting and daydreaming by the lake. Look around you. There is no storm. Tell me now, what's bothering you?'

Narada stared around him, flabbergasted, and told Vishnu the whole story.

The lord finally admitted, 'I am the one who created that maya for you. You are neither married nor do you have children. Maybe now you can understand what attachment feels like and how hard it is for the common man to be detached from it all. If an accomplished sage like you can get caught in this web of illusion, just imagine how others must cope with it. Your father is absolutely right, dear devotee.'

Narada bowed his head in shame.

Vishnu smiled. 'I want people to remember this unique incident, and so the names of your sixty children will represent each of the upcoming sixty years or *samvatsaras*. At the end of sixty years, the cycle will repeat itself.'

This is how the Indian calendar or samvatsara came into existence.

The Debt for a Wedding

One day, the sage Kashyapa was performing a yagna on the banks of the Ganga with other ascetics when Narada, the wanderer of the realms, visited them. Narada asked the group, 'O respected sages, which god are you aiming to please with this ritual?'

There was no consensus among the sages, so they asked the sage Bhrigu to visit Brahma, Vishnu and Shiva and find out which god would be pleased with their worship.

First, Bhrigu went to Satyaloka, the abode of Brahma. There, he observed Brahma and Saraswati, who were busy reciting the Vedas. Without drawing attention to himself, he quietly left and made his way to Mount Kailash. When he reached the mountaintop, he found Shiva and Parvati deep in meditation. Finally, he made his way to Vaikuntha, the home of Vishnu.

When he reached Vaikuntha, Bhrigu saw Vishnu resting on the snake Adisesha. The goddess Lakshmi was at Vishnu's feet, completely entranced by her consort. Sage Bhrigu became upset. The god was not doing anything useful. In fact, he had not even noticed the sage! Growing angry,

Bhrigu came forward and kicked Vishnu on the left side of
his chest.

Vishnu was known to be gentle to his devotees. His
response to the kick was to just get up and press Bhrigu's
leg, as if to appease him. The real reason, however, was
something else. Vishnu knew that Bhrigu had a powerful eye
under his feet, which caused the sage to behave aggressively.
Under the pretext of pressing Bhrigu's feet, Vishnu had taken
away the extra eye. Immediately, Bhrigu's demeanour changed;
he calmed down and apologized to the god. At that moment,
Bhrigu realized that Vishnu would be the god who would be
most pleased with the yagna by the river.

After Bhrigu departed to tell the other sages, Lakshmi
turned to Vishnu, her irritation obvious. 'I know your devotees
are dear to you, my lord,' she said, 'but you must see to it
that they don't take you for granted. Bhrigu may be a great
man, but what he did was wrong and you didn't even give
him a piece of your mind.'

Vishnu tried to pacify her and tell her about Bhrigu's
third eye, but Lakshmi refused to hear him out. 'Bhrigu
kicked you on the left side of your chest and that's where I
reside—in your heart. How do you expect me to continue
staying there?'

Hurt and upset, Lakshmi went away to a place called
Karvirapura.

Without Lakshmi, Vishnu was rather lonely in Vaikuntha
and so he went down to earth, to the kingdom of Chola.
He took shelter inside a huge cave-like structure under
a tamarind tree on a hilltop, without realizing that he had
entered an enormous anthill. Soon, he began to meditate

without food or sleep. In time, an anthill mound developed around him.[11]

Meanwhile, Brahma and Shiva felt sorry for Vishnu and decided to make sure he at least had something to drink. So they took the form of a cow and a calf and joined Chola's herd of cows, grazing on the same hill where Vishnu was meditating.

When the royal cowherd took the cows to the hill, the cow and the calf made their way to the anthill. The cow deliberately began dripping milk through the visible holes in the anthill and Vishnu ended up drinking the milk that trickled into his mouth.

After a few days, the kitchen staff became quite concerned. Whenever they wanted to milk the new cow, they found that her udders were empty! The cowherd was worried that people would start to think he was stealing milk from the new cow, and so he decided to follow the beast while she was grazing.

The next morning, he let the cow out and stealthily tracked her from a distance. As usual, the cow placed her udders on top of the anthill, and milk freely flowed into it. The cowherd, who had been watching from behind a bush, was enraged. He brought out his axe and ran towards the cow with the intent of cutting off her head. Realizing the danger despite being in meditation, Vishnu rose from the anthill to save the cow. The herdsman was caught off guard and, in his panic, dropped the axe on Vishnu's forehead

---

[11] Today, the hills where Vishnu meditated are called the Tirumala Hills and the area below has come to be known as Govindarajpatnam, or Tirupati.

before collapsing on the ground and dying of shock. The god's forehead began bleeding and the cow returned to the palace with bloodstains on her body.

When word of the cow's blood-streaked body reached the king, he knew that something was amiss and so he let the cow loose again and tracked her just as the cowherd had done. The cow returned to the anthill out of habit. The king recognized Vishnu in his human form.

Vishnu, however, was extremely distressed. 'O king, your royal cowherd—the protector of the cows—was ready to kill one from his very own herd. Since he was your servant, as his superior, you are responsible for his errors, and so you will be punished. You will be reborn as an asura in your next birth.'

The king pleaded his innocence and eventually, Vishnu took pity on him. He said, 'After you complete your punishment, you will be reborn as another king—Akasha Raja.'

Vishnu then left the kingdom and began wandering in the forests.

After more than a century, his prophecy came true. King Akasha Raja was born to rule over a kingdom known as Tondamandalam. The king had everything except what he wanted the most—a child to call his own. Finally, he decided to perform a yagna. As part of the ritual, the king had to plough a few fields. The moment the king touched the plough, it transformed into a huge, beautiful lotus. When he examined the magical lotus, he was delighted to find a baby girl inside. 'See what the lord has blessed us with,' he said to his wife. 'We will name her Padmavati, or "the one who emerged from the lotus".'

The years flew by and Padmavati grew up to be a fine princess.

By now. Vishnu had a different name—Srinivasa—and he would always be found wandering the seven hills of Tondamandalam.

In this form, Vishnu met a lady named Bakula Devi. As soon as she saw Srinivasa, she felt a wave of maternal affection for him. Srinivasa smiled and agreed to become her child, because she was a reincarnation of Yashoda, the foster mother of Krishna.

Though Yashoda had raised Krishna in her original life, she had not seen any of his eight marriages, a fact that had greatly upset her. And Krishna had promised her that she would be responsible for his marriage in one of his births.

One day, Srinivasa went hunting on Venkatadri, one of the seven hills. While he was chasing a wild elephant, he happened to reach the royal gardens, where Padmavati and her friends were picking flowers. The wild elephant ran past the gardens and disappeared from sight, even as the maidens screamed. The sight of the elephant had scared the princess and her companions.

When Srinivasa entered the gardens, still in pursuit of the elephant, the maidens thought that he was a trespasser, and so they threw stones at him. Srinivasa, however, was not the least bit concerned about the elephant by then. He had fallen in love with Padmavati the moment he had lain eyes on her and wanted to marry her. And unknown to him, Padmavati had also taken a fancy to this mysterious stranger.

Srinivasa left the gardens and ran back home to tell his mother about the beautiful princess and his intention to marry her. After listening to his declaration of love for Padmavati, Bakula Devi agreed to help him. She offered to visit the king and queen and request for the princess's hand in marriage on behalf of her son, but Srinivasa had to be patient and wait a while.

Meanwhile, Padmavati could not get the handsome stranger out of her mind. She did not know anything about him, and she was too shy to tell her parents about her feelings. Days passed and the princess became depressed. As a result, her health started to deteriorate.

Bakula Devi disguised herself as a soothsayer and staged a chance meeting with Padmavati and her friends. Padmavati's friends told the soothsayer that the princess was pining for a handsome stranger and insisted that she foretell the princess's future.

'She will marry the man she loves and he will be the most deserving of her,' predicted the soothsayer.

A few days later, Bakula Devi visited the palace as herself and convinced the king and queen to give Padmavati's hand in marriage to Srinivasa. And the wedding was fixed!

Everybody wanted to attend the auspicious ceremony, but Srinivasa had no wealth because Lakshmi had long left him. Kubera, the god of wealth, offered to loan the money for the wedding. And so Srinivasa and Padmavati were married in a grand celebration held in Narayanavanam.

At the wedding, Lakshmi came to bless the couple and said to Srinivasa, 'Please don't worry about the loan. I will forever reside in the homes of all your devotees, who will later help you repay the loan.'

According to our scriptures, there are many yugas (or eras), out of which Kali yuga is the last one. When Kali yuga eventually arrived, Srinivasa wanted to return to his abode but all the rishis pleaded with him to stay through the dangerous yuga and protect everyone from the hilltop. Princess Padmavati chose not to accompany her husband and stayed back. She is popularly known as Alamelumanga and depicted as an auspicious deity sitting on a lotus.

Vishnu, however, went up to Seshadri Hill. The hill belonged to a deity known as Varahaswami, who was concerned that everyone would worship the more popular Srinivasa instead of him. But Vishnu promised him that all the devotees would first visit Varahaswami's temple before visiting Tirumala.

Vishnu turned into a stone statue with four hands. He carried the shankha in one hand, the chakra in the second, while the palm of his third hand faced downward—with the front depicting Vaikuntha—and the fourth was balled into a fist. Srinivasa also came to be known as Venkateshwara because he was now considered to be the lord of the hill Venkatadri.

There is a belief that Venkateshwara turned into a statue before he could pay back Kubera's loan. His devotees, having decided to help him repay his debt, make huge donations to the present-day Tirupati temple. Apparently the amount of money loaned was so huge that the sum being collected from the devotees visiting the temple every day is still only paying the interest on the principal amount. Legend has it that Govindaraja, a deity who was Venkateshwara's foster brother, used to measure the money received in huge pots. However, he grew tired of this job and fell asleep. So he also turned into a statue! His statue can be seen in Govindarajpatnam.

There is also a statue of Lakshmi, depicted with open palms. It appears as though she is blessing the devotees with wealth. The statue is located next to a *hundi*, or money pot, and all devotees bow before her and ask for her favour.

Every year, the Padmavati and Lakshmi temples receive saris as gifts from Lord Venkateshwara.

The Tirumala temple and its deity have been worshipped for thousands of years, and many kings, queens, princes and princesses have donated generously to develop the temple. Several different styles of architecture have been added to the original temple over the years and can still be viewed today. Many songs have been composed in Vishnu's glory. Srinivasa (also called Balaji) attracts people from all over India. Devotees believe that one glance at the statue of Venkateshwara is a wondrous moment because it is but the real god in the form of a statue. The number of people visiting the deity and donating to the temple range from 65,000 a day to about five lakhs during festivals. This is what has made Kubera, the treasurer of the gods, one of the richest beings in the world.

Karvirapura is better known today as Kolhapur. It is believed that Lakshmi continues to reside there.

One of the seven hills of Tondamandalam is now named Garudadri because of its resemblance to Garuda.

Padmavati was a reincarnation of Vedavati, a pious woman who had performed an intense penance out of her desire to wed Rama. Rama had said to her, 'Vedavati, I cannot marry you in this lifetime. But I promise that you will be my wife in another.'

The Asura and the Super-God

Guha was an asura and a great devotee of Lord Brahma. Like most asuras, he wanted to live forever and prayed to Brahma in the hope of attaining immortality. Brahma eventually appeared in front of him, but before Guha could utter his wish, the god said, 'Guheshwara, please don't ask me for immortality! Anything but that!'

'Lord, then bless me with such a boon that will ensure that I can't be killed by anyone—neither god nor human,' replied Guha. He knew that if the gods couldn't kill him, then nobody could.

'So be it,' said Brahma.

Guha soon became the king of the asuras and defeated all those who opposed him. He even tormented learned men and scholars. There was no peace in the land—only chaos reigned.

People prayed to Shiva and Vishnu for help. 'What a boon he has been given! Please relieve us of this anguish. Either kill him or kill us. We cannot bear to live in this land any more!'

Shiva and Vishnu assured the devotees that they would take care of the matter and tried to come up with a plan. There was no easy solution as Brahma had decreed that even the gods could not defeat Guha!

Then Vishnu had an idea. He said to Shiva, 'What if we join our bodies? Then we are not one god, but two! And with your might and my mind, perhaps we can slay Guha?'

Shiva agreed.

And so the right side of Shiva—with the crescent moon, River Ganga, the trident, the damru and half of his third eye—joined with Vishnu's left side, which had the chakra, the gada, his crown and Garuda.

The new being was called Harihara and once he was formed, this super-god made his way straight to Guha, who ran away in terror. But Harihara soon managed to catch him on the banks of River Tungabhadra. Guha surrendered and said, 'I know I won't survive this, but I have one last desire. Please let me be under your holy feet.'

So Harihara brought down one foot on the asura's head and he entered the lower realm, thus relieving the earth of the demonic presence.

This super-god Harihareshwara is worshipped by devotees of both Shiva and Vishnu. In the eleventh century, a temple carved out of stone was built by the Hoysala kings. The temple contains the statue of Shankar Narayana or Harihara, and displays the features and qualities of both Shiva and Vishnu. Today, the town of Harihara stands near the Tungabhadra.

Notes

Gods and Their Abodes

Deva or Asura	Abode (Ancient Name)	Abode (Modern Name)
Brahma	Pushkar	Pushkar
	Brahma Kapala	Badrinath
	Satyaloka	
Shiva	Mount Kailash	Mount Kailash
	Kashi	Varanasi or Benares
Vishnu	Vaikuntha	
	Tondamandalam	Around Tirupati
Lakshmi	Karvirapura	Kolhapur
Indra	Indraloka / Amravati	
Ravana	Lanka	Sri Lanka

Jyotirlingas

Name	Place	State
Somnath	Prabhas Patan, Saurashtra	Gujarat
Nagesha	Darukawana	Gujarat

Name	Place	State
Mallikarjuna	Srisailam	Andhra Pradesh
Mahakala	Ujjain	Madhya Pradesh
Amaleshwara	Omkara	Madhya Pradesh
Vaijanatha	Paraji	Maharashtra
Bhimashankara	Bhimashankara	Maharashtra
Trumbakeshwara	Nashik	Maharashtra
Grishneshwara	Ellora	Maharashtra
Rameswaram	Rameswaram	Tamil Nadu
Vishweshwara	Kashi	Uttar Pradesh
Kedareshwara	Kedar	Uttaranchal

Immortality Loopholes

Devotee	Boon	Loophole
Sunda and Upasunda	Cannot be killed by anyone but each other	Died fighting each other over a beautiful maiden
Taraka	Cannot be killed by any man or god	Died at the hands of a child, Shiva's son
Tripurasuras	To be rulers of three invincible cities, whose weakest moment would occur during their alignment once every thousand years	A single arrow used by Shiva during the alignment
Gajasura	Cannot be killed by anyone who desires something	Destroyed by Lord Shiva, who desires nothing in the world

Devotee	Boon	Loophole
Vritrasura	Cannot be killed by any weapon made of wood or metal	Slain by weapons made from the bones of the sage Dadhichi
Hiranyakashipu	Cannot be killed by a human or an animal, in the morning or at night, inside or outside the house	Killed by a half-man, half-lion at twilight in a doorway
Jalandhara	Cannot be destroyed by anyone other than Shiva, who was like his father	Died at the hands of Shiva
Madhu and Kaitabha	Can choose the time of their death	Chose to die after Vishnu obtained a boon from them asking them to die at his hands
Guha	Cannot be killed by a man or a god	Was killed by two gods merging to form a deity, Harihara

READ MORE BY SUDHA MURTY

The Serpent's Revenge
Unusual Tales from the Mahabharata

How many names does Arjuna have?
Why was Yama cursed?
What lesson did a little mongoose teach Yudhisthira?

The Kurukshetra war, fought between the Kauravas and the Pandavas and which forced even the gods to take sides, may be well known, but there are innumerable stories set before, after and during the war that lend the Mahabharata its many varied shades and are largely unheard of.

Award-winning author Sudha Murty reintroduces the fascinating world of India's greatest epic through the extraordinary tales in this collection, each of which is sure to fill you with a sense of wonder and bewilderment.

READ MORE BY SUDHA MURTY

The Magic of the Lost Temple

City girl Nooni is surprised at the pace of life in her grandparents' village in Karnataka. But she quickly gets used to the gentle routine there and involves herself in a flurry of activities, including papad making, organizing picnics and learning to ride a cycle, with her new-found friends. Things get exciting when Nooni stumbles upon an ancient fabled stepwell right in the middle of a forest.

Join the intrepid Nooni on an adventure of a lifetime in this much-awaited book by Sudha Murty that is heart-warming, charming and absolutely unputdownable